I0770831

DEATH IN THE LAKE DISTRICT

A WARM SPRINGS MYSTERY

BOOK THREE

D. SMITH

Death in the Lake District by D. Smith

Book 3 in the Warm Springs Mystery series

Published by Kingfisher Press

Fairview, North Carolina, United States of America

Visit the author's website at www.douglaspsmith.com

Copyright © 2025 Douglas P. Smith

All rights reserved. No portion of this book may be reproduced in any form without permission from the publisher, except as permitted by U.S. copyright law. For permissions contact: thekingfisherpress@gmail.com

Cover design by Getcovers

Print ISBN: 978-1-964344-05-8

This book is a work of fiction. Names, characters, places, and incidents are either the product of the author's imagination or are used fictitiously. Any resemblance to actual persons, living or dead, or to actual events or locales is entirely coincidental.

My phone rang, and I looked at the screen. I rarely answered calls anymore unless I knew the caller, and I felt like it. Today's call satisfied neither requirement. Not only was it a number I didn't recognize, it was an unusual format and one I had not seen in a while. I immediately registered the +44 prefix in front of 4 digits, a space, then six digits as a call from the UK. It had been a few years and a career ago since any business associates had called me from there. I held the phone for a minute to see if there was a voicemail notification, but there was not. I filed it under mildly interesting, pocketed the phone, and went back to hacking weeds out of the community garden. There were about twenty more minutes of manual labor before the chore was finished.

Back home after a shower, I fixed dinner and sat on the porch. I thought about calling Donna, but I was not sure she was back and recovered from her book tour yet. She had been on a driving tour around the southeast, mostly in towns and small cities. Then she ended the tour with large shows in Atlanta and Dallas. It sounded like more fun than it was. A new town and a new hotel every night, with a reading and book signing every day. It would be tedious, but it was necessary to keep her readers satiated.

She had not asked me to go, and I was grateful for her not asking. I missed her, but she probably knew the trip would not be fun. We still spent time together, but neither of us had figured out where this relationship was going. Or maybe she had, but not told me yet. I was usually the last to know about any relationship status. Warm Springs was so small that a dozen people might know before I did.

Otherwise, life had gotten quiet again after the kerfuffle with the rogue sheriff and the vicious tow truck driver. The sheriff was doing twenty years in prison for his drug operation, along with two of his deputies, and Doyle the car tower was dead. The county was now a better place regarding both outcomes. Plus the California boutique pot grower, also involved with both the sheriff and Doyle Vickers, had gone back to the West Coast.

Millard and his gang of octogenarian sleuths had given me credit for solving Mike Vickers' murder and pinning it on Doyle. There had not been a confession before he was killed, but all the evidence pointed at Doyle. Evidence proved his warehouse was where Mike was shot, and Doyle's truck that was spotted on camera at the body dump site tested positive for Mike's DNA. There was just one problem with that scenario, and something I would need to tell Bryan about, eventually.

It was a nice early fall day, too nice to think about past murders. I decided a walk was in my future, so I asked Kat for permission to leave. She did not respond at first, then got up and trilled on the way to the refrigerator. That was my cue to bribe her acquiescence with roast chicken. That done, I was on my way.

Passing the once beautiful, now rotting cottages along the outer loop of the campus always gave me a feeling of despair. Part of the Roosevelt Warm Springs, or RWS, campus, the cottages had been built anywhere from 70 to 98 years ago for people living and working on campus. But once the owners left the cottages were held empty and abandoned by the state, since they remained state property. A lot of history and aesthetic architecture were slowly turning to dust.

As I made my way along the outer loop road, I came to one of the cottages that was in private ownership and still inhabited. My friend Millard, more than eighty years old, made it his kingdom. The side-by-side utility vehicle, street legal at least in Warm Springs, was out front, so he was home. I had given it to him so he could get around easier on and off campus with his bad hip. He stepped out the door and onto his porch with a pitcher of something resembling lemonade. I was right on time.

"James, come up and have a shot of vitamin C," he said.

"Thanks Millard, I believe I will."

We sat in the rocking chairs and enjoyed the sweet-sour lemonade on ice. Just one sprig of mint to give it the slightest hint of exotic.

"You've been awfully quiet these days," Millard said. "No murder, mayhem, or ruckus at all that you've been associated with. Makes me think you are planning something."

"Millard, all I'm planning is how to make more money from a bookstore and what to plant next in the campus community garden."

"That is terribly boring. Not even a wedding on the horizon?" I gave him my best withering look. It didn't work. "Poor girl didn't throw you over for some wealthy baseball player, did she? Or find a match out on her tour?"

"Not that I am aware of. We are still seeing each other. But like everything else lately, it's been slow."

"The shiny days have worn off and you don't know what to do with the patina, now do you?"

"Never heard it put quite like that, but maybe so."

"You will need to jumpstart those lusty urges back to the early days. Before she got to see your used toothbrush."

"Thanks for your input, but that is not the problem."

"Then what is? You can tell old Uncle Millard. Sometimes I might even give you good advice."

"I'm not really sure. She's a great person and wonderful company. The problem is me."

"Oh, got it. You don't think you are worthy, or are you looking to shop at another supermarket?"

"Neither. I think I'm bored, floating in the doldrums of life at the moment. Not even Donna has pulled me out, and it's certainly not her duty to do so anyway."

"Have you told her?"

"No, but I think she knows something is wrong. Although it is not like anything is wrong, except for my attitude."

"You best get to talking to her. As a woman, she might think you've lost interest in her, so she will protect her emotions. You will be on the outs because you have a pouty attitude. Dumb way to lose her."

"I have to admit you are right. She should be home and rested up from the tour. As soon as I finish the lemonade, I'm going to start walking and give her a call."

"Don't wait. There is always more lemonade where this came from. But there aren't that many nice people out there who like you."

"Excellent point. Thanks Millard, I'll be going now."

"Good luck and don't screw it up. Can't have you moping all over my porch now that I have a social life."

I believe he was giving me the bum's rush because he had company coming over or had a date in town. When I got to the end of his driveway, I called Donna.

"Hi there. Do you have time to talk?"

"Hi James. On the phone or somewhere else?"

"Somewhere else. Anywhere you would like."

"How about your front porch? I need something quiet after the last three weeks."

"Sounds great."

"I'll be there in thirty minutes."

I was already feeling better. Now I just had to decide how to tell Donna I was floating in a dead zone that had nothing to do with her.

I had put out two cold drinks on the porch when

Donna drove up. She gave me a quick peck more reminiscent of a friend than anything more. Maybe I had waited too long.

"Thanks for coming over."

"Sure James. It sounded like you needed to talk."

"I do. I stopped by to see Millard while out walking. He asked me what was wrong. I wasn't sure or really even realized anything was. But I knew he was right, that I might be acting off."

"You are definitely off. I think it started about two months ago. Almost to the point I was going to say something, but I decided to wait until after I got back."

"You noticed too?"

"Of course I did. So what is wrong?"

"I feel like I'm slightly adrift. Not much is happening at the bookstore. My daily life is wonderful yet not very exciting."

"I suspect you are a bit of an adventure junky. But you now live in a tiny town with little happening, and own one of the least adventurous businesses known to humankind."

"What do I do to break out of the slump?"

"You need more excitement. Even more than what I can provide as your girlfriend."

"Are you my girlfriend?"

"I believe so. All the facts point toward it being true. Do you want to be my boyfriend?"

"I think so."

She made a bad buzzer noise. "Brrruurrzzz. Wrong answer. You have one more chance."

"Yes, I want to. But I don't know how to make it work."

"You don't make it work. We make it work, up to the

point that one or both of us would rather floss with barbed wire than keep going."

"In that case, as my official girlfriend, I now entrust you with exciting me."

"You know how lame that sounds, right?"

"I do, but it was so bad I really needed to say it."

"Let's get you to an adventure, preferably one where you don't have to talk. It does not have to be a murder, does it? I'm fresh out of those, thankfully."

"Awww, I was hoping for murder. But mayhem would do nicely."

"What have you done for excitement in the past? There must have been something you enjoyed before chasing murderers."

"In my younger days I went hunting and fishing. Then I realized how silly and sad that was. Not for me but for the dead animals that resulted. Other things have come and gone. Maybe the only thing left in my external life is travel. Have you ever been to Alaska?"

"I have not but always wanted to go. Are you asking me?"

"I believe so. Or are there other places you would like to go?"

"I have a long list. I traveled some while married and liked it. I would like to go see the western US, Alaska, several Caribbean islands, and just about anywhere in Europe."

"Not Hawaii?"

"Been there on a former honeymoon. Liked it but don't need to go back until I've seen everything else on the list."

"I feel the same way. Nice, but there are lots of other places to go."

"Let me think on it a while. I'll come up with a top-five list, and you do the same. If we have matches, we can set up a trip."

"I like that. It sounds so mature that two people can make rational decisions."

"Keep that mature talk to yourself. I'm still thirty-nine."

"Do you have any minimum requirements?"

"Someplace that does not require prior immunizations, and wherever we go I need a fully functional bathroom with shower."

"I can go along with that. Somewhere with adequate facilities and no epidemics. I'll add jungle to the do not go list. Heat, humidity, bugs and snakes don't sound fun."

"Me either. The jungle would not be good for my hair. Now, will a trip get you back to normal?"

"Can't hurt as it should reset my dour meter."

"Yes, let's have all that dour go away. But to reset my dour meter, what kind of dinner can you feed me?"

"I'll find something to make you happy. If I didn't know better, I'd think you wanted to meet here so you could persuade me to fix you dinner."

"You know better, and that's exactly why we met here. I have not had a decent home-cooked meal in weeks."

"Well then, I will make something worthy to welcome you back."

"Thank you, James. Now get to it, and how can I help?"

CHAPTER TWO

Looking at my phone ringing, I saw it was the same UK number as before. Possibly a recruiter who had not gotten the notice the past years that I was not interested in any position they might offer. Persistent, however. Again, I didn't answer, as a second call fell under a new criteria. If it was really important, they would call again, or maybe leave a voicemail that I could delete. I held the phone, but again there was no voicemail notification. Back to writing and petting Kat. I still could not think of who would call me from the UK. To satisfy my curiosity, I put the number into a search engine on my computer. If it was an official line from a corporation, it should return a hit. But there was no valid search result, so probably a cell phone.

I put it out of my mind as I needed to refresh myself on training materials I had not looked at in more than two years. I had volunteered to give a food safety training to the cafeteria staff, and tomorrow was the day. Doubtful they needed it, but the state required it as a step toward allowing them to use the garden vegetables and greens on the salad bar. As I went through the material, it came back quickly, as I had dealt with it for forty years. At least for me, it was simple. Cook whatever needed to be cooked and don't recontaminate it. Keep everything cold, clean, and moving through the kitchen. Wash hands a lot. Never eat or serve suspect food. Everything else was a series of details specific to each food, including a newer chapter on human allergies.

I met the staff the next morning in a conference room in the Georgia Hall. Millard had the bookstore today, and Kat was at home. At lunch I'd go home and unleash her on the horde of chipmunks. Meanwhile, I had the pleasure of boring the cafeteria staff with all the details of food safety. I broke up the morning session with horror stories and a few funny ones I had run into over the years. They had a few of their own. We broke for lunch, and most of the staff wandered back to their kitchen to help out. I had half of the staff in the morning, then the other half in the afternoon. To cope with the labor shortage, they were serving a limited menu for lunch and dinner.

The afternoon session went much as the morning had. I hated boring people by telling them information they already knew and used daily. I tried to keep it light and continue telling stories, and asking about their experiences. They had all been to mandatory training before, so they knew how the game worked. They were a captive audience, so I felt even more inclined to make it less boring.

Thankfully, for all involved, it was over. George and his staff left to give the dinner staff a hand. I'm sure they would quickly implement the knowledge and wisdom I had imparted. Which was exactly equal to what they already knew. I walked back to my house. It was still unseasonably hot for fall. Too warm to risk the ticks and snakes to go up the back way to Pine Mountain. I did two circuits of the outer loop and then went downhill to the former golf course.

George and Wes were already there at the garden, then Edna drove up. Robert came last with Alicia and baby Alice. Our job today was take in the last of the corn and tomatoes. Another week and they would be plowed under. We checked the pumpkin vines which were growing nicely, and everyone was looking forward to pumpkins this year. We also began preparing a fallow area for winter crops. This fall, the cabbage would be planted. Possibly other cool-season crops, but we had not decided which ones yet. Last, we dug up a row of potatoes. A bushel for the cafeteria, and each of us took two handfuls for home.

The garden was slowly becoming a campus favorite. People were now asking about it, and some were likely to volunteer soon. I imagine they were waiting for cooler weather, as the Warm Springs heat during the day had not yet diminished. It was good to see Robert working with

Alisha. He had started coming with her every other week. With the two of them, they could look after Alice as she was now walking and more likely to want out of her play area. We didn't want her eating grasshoppers or dirt on our watch.

I walked home to get a bite and share some chicken with Kat. As always, I got white meat, and she got dark. Another one of our compatibilities. The day was still hot, so we both stayed on the porch in the shade. I knew as soon as the sun dropped she would be off on her rounds between the woods and the house. I kept a closer watch on her as a grey fox had moved in. Literally. He or she was now living in the abandoned cottage across the street. So far there had been no trouble as the small fox had not shown any inclination to get into a tussle with Kat or the other strays on campus. I realized that every stray cat and the fox could each have their own cottage for shelter. There were lots of squirrels and other creatures for food sources, and I suspect some people on campus were feeding the animals. Whatever the reason, the feral cats did not fight among themselves or with the fox or Kat.

The rest of the evening was quiet. I traded texts with Donna and made plans with Sam and Irene to have lunch the following week. Soon they would be off on a "vacation" to Maine to load up the camper with edible marijuana products. It was part of their business and kept a lot of elderly Hamilton County residents feeling better and more mobile. I was thinking I might join those ranks soon enough. My mind felt young, but my body had some miles on it. I settled in for the evening with Kat in the chair getting her belly rub.

I made the cafeteria early the next morning since I was due to open the bookstore. I really needed a morning assistant. Someone to get up early, open the store, sell tons of books, and work for free. I knew better than to post that job position. Someone might actually apply, and then I'd have to explain it was a hoax.

I noticed Ison at his usual table. After choosing eggs and grits, I moved in his direction. Breakfast was a travesty without bacon or sausage, but I was skipping meat every other day for the dubious purpose of better health. Good thing I had not gotten on the marijuana gummy kick or I'd probably have eaten the whole pan of bacon.

"Hi Ison, mind if I sit?"

"Morning James, please join me. Oh, that's too bad. Breakfast without pork. You poor thing."

"I feel the same way. But something good may come from it?"

"Like what?"

"I honestly don't know. It seemed like a good idea, but now I can't think why."

"Your brain cells have broken down without the morning protein supplement. Next thing you know, you will stop drinking coffee and we will have to wheel you in for shock treatments."

"I thought those were no longer allowed."

"True, but yours would be a special exception. Lots of people would want to pull that handle. We could even sell raffle tickets."

"Go ahead if it is for a good cause. Who do you think would be first in line?"

"Oh, that would be Benjamin Rawley. Just this week I

heard him curse your name once again. Seriously though, he is looking to do something. I imagine he's petty enough to get the community campus garden project stopped."

"I can't believe the documents on the campus cottage scam did not get him fired last year. If he tries to sabotage the garden, I might have to resort to alternative methods."

"I've heard his latest project is to get approval to clear-cut the trees on campus."

"I could see that. You'll remember it was part of the scam that Joe the real estate agent set up with Benjamin. They'd have one of their buddies cut the trees for the condo development, then cut as many others on campus as possible without permission. A small part of the scam, all of which was illegal."

"He's back at it. Never one to let a bad idea fade away, especially if he can profit from it. But he should have learned from Joe's death, which you caused, that things don't always go as planned."

"Ison, you've convinced me he needs to be stopped. I don't know how yet, but I'm pretty sure I know who can help with that."

"Please proceed, with all haste. Campus would be a better place without the Benjamin blight."

"I'll see what I can do."

The morning started off poorly with the news about Benjamin's shenanigans. I put Kat on the bike and pedaled to the bookstore on my Dutch bike, the Grey Ghost. I opened the door. Kat went on her rounds while I changed the sign to Open for the day. Over time, I had just a tiny bit less excitement when I opened the door each day. But I could not imagine walking away from it.

The slow morning of a few customers was underperformed by the lack of any in the afternoon. I had brought lunch, so I did not go next door to Mable's Diner. Kat was not impressed with her portion of roast chicken. I could almost hear her thinking she could have gotten that at home; she needed something like ham from next door. She probably ate better than most of the cats in the county, so she could throw shade at my offering if she wanted to, but it was all she would get. Half an hour later I noticed it was gone. She had stealthily come back and eaten it after initially rejecting it. She had made her point and still gotten lunch.

I finished up my exciting foray into state sales tax computations. The only benefit of few sales was keeping up with the taxes. I checked over inventory and reviewed upcoming new releases from the publishers. My personal assistant, which was me with a higher-pitched voice, asked Kat if she was ready to go home and end the workday early. I got a trill and decided it was affirmative. Then it was on the bike and back home.

CHAPTER THREE

Again, the UK number was showing on my vibrating phone. Three calls from a probable cell that I didn't know. My number was out in the wild, unfortunately. Maybe it was from an agency or someone who actually read something I once wrote. I decided to take a chance. What was the worst thing that could happen?

"Hello."

Silence, then, "James?"

It was my turn for silence as I could not believe what or rather who I had heard. The worst might actually be happening.

"James, are you there?" The voice was one I once yearned to hear every day, then despised for a long time once I didn't hear it. After that, it was a voice I was sure I'd never hear again. Yet here it was, emerging from the glass screen on my phone.

"Yes, I'm here. Just confused."

"Is this a bad time?"

Oh my, was it ever. It had been for more than thirty years. "No more than usual. I'm …" I did not finish the sentence because I had no words formed in my brain.

"Surprised to hear from me?" She could always finish my sentences. With her low-pitched lilt infused with a Lancashire accent that I once found attractive. She sounded the same, but her voice was thinner. Maybe because it lacked some of the passion it once did. Although the simplest explanation was that she was much older than the last time I had heard her voice.

"You have no idea," I answered.

"I didn't know if you would take my call. I had tried a few times before."

"I nearly didn't since I don't normally answer unknown numbers." I might have said that a bit more strongly than intended. Too much emphasis on the last words of the sentence. She must have picked up on my inflection.

"I knew this would not be easy. It has been too long."

"You are the one that said you would never contact me again. Twice, as I remember, in France."

"I know."

I had nothing left to say. Half a decade of anger, a near-decade of a sense of loss, and two decades of blessed silence as I had too many other things and more important people to think of. Now I was getting hit with a barrage of thoughts and emotions I had never expected to experience.

"James, are you going to talk to me? I… James… I need help."

That last was said with a tremor. My brain was not working right. I was living a Salvador Dali painting; reality was melting around me. I bailed, still not having any useful words to say.

"I have to go. I'll call you back." I disconnected the line. I leaned over to let my head clear. I was having a bad reaction to the experience of having my ex-wife calling me after nearly thirty-five years of silence.

Five minutes later I was once again functional, and my head was clear. Well, slightly clearer than before. I put my emotions back into the screaming, squirming cellar where they had erupted from and closed the door. I mentally went through my usual list of curse words. If I said them silently, then surely it did not count against me.

Now that my logical brain was back online and functioning, what did I know? Nothing really. She called out of the blue and asked for help. Then I figuratively ran off like a scalded cat. It was time to act like an adult. I pulled up the recent calls and tapped the number.

"Hullow, James?"

"Hi. Sorry about my abrupt departure. I had to get my wits in order after the initial shock."

"I understand. I never thought to be ringing you."

"Now I'm normal and can listen to you. What is happening?"

"There's been some trouble. It is a very long tale, lots of

turns and twists. But there has been a death, and I'm a suspect."

"I'm not sure what to say. I'm not a lawyer or official investigator, so what do you need me for?"

"I'm afraid it is a lot to ask. Considering everything… But is there any way you can come here for a few days to help me sort this out? I have no one else to ask."

"Where?"

"Keswick." Hearing the name of the town was a last shock to the system. But I needed to get through this and find out what I could.

"Is there any research I can do beforehand?"

"Not that I can think of."

"I'll try to be there soon, depending on flights."

"Really? Thank you."

"I'll text you at this number when I get to Windermere."

"I appreciate this, James. You don't know how much."

"I'll see you soon." I ended the call.

Was I really daft enough to do this? Maybe. Online, I found a plane ticket to Manchester and a train ticket from the airport station to the town of Windermere. It was easy enough to do, but should I? An internal voice was telling me to call her back and cancel. Helping a friend or family member and it would have been an automatic yes. But an ex-wife in another country after decades of no contact was not the same. To decide, I turned it around. If I were a suspect in a death and needed help, how desperate would I have to be to call her? Extremely desperate, apparently. I would go.

I set up the trip and reserved tickets for the flight, train, and then the bus to Keswick. I had not driven in the UK in decades and did not trust my skills for driving on the wrong side of the road. I would probably catch on quickly enough unless I got a stick shift instead of an automatic transmission with the rental. I easily drove a manual in America, but using my left hand to change gears in the UK drove me crazy. Killing myself and possibly others was not in my plans.

I made two calls and got Kat settled with people to feed and stay with her a bit each day for up to two weeks. Other than that, I did not have many loose ends to worry about. I called Millard, and he was happy to watch the store. That gave me time to think about what I was doing again. Jumping on a plane to go overseas to meet up with an ex-wife from decades ago because she said she needed help was fraught with issues. But I knew so little I needed to play this straight. Go over, listen to her, help if I could, and come home. Worst case, I got a trip to a place I loved to visit.

But why did it have to be Keswick, in the Lake District? That had been our happiest time together. A few red flags sprouted as my savior complex popped up, along with the possible manipulation gambit, and of course the memory enshrinement. People don't stay the same after that many years, and we were a lifetime apart. But curiosity about her and what was happening in her life was one reason. Also, despite my serene life on the Roosevelt campus I had been bored lately. Not much was happening on campus, in town or the county. I could use a change, and obviously those around me, like Millard and Donna, had seen it too.

Oops, I remembered very recently asking Donna about going to Alaska or somewhere similar. Now I was planning on flying off to the UK on a moment's notice. Worse, it was to see my ex-wife. Explaining this was going to be tricky. Perhaps suicidal if Donna was holding anything sharp when I told her. For a brief second I thought about asking Donna to go with me. The thought dropped into the hole it deserved on the next second. I would not be able to enjoy a trip with Donna if I was working on a case for my former spouse. Both Donna and the case would get short-changed. I did not think Donna would even consider going with me since she was intelligent and practical. Perhaps I should have adopted the same two parameters before agreeing to go.

I needed to explain fully to Donna what I was doing. I should probably think about the "why" aspect before having that conversation. Otherwise it would be an even more awkward discussion. I was not sure even my cooking skills would get me a pass from Donna in this case. No reason to delay, so I called and asked her over.

An hour later and it was time for me dive into treacherous waters.

"Hi Donna. Thanks for coming."

"James you look like you have seen a ghost. What is going on?"

"I have not seen one, but I did just hear from one. Sort of. I need to talk to you about it."

"Sure go ahead. Do we need drinks?"

"Maybe. What would you like?"

"Depends on the coming conversation. You know more than I do. Wine or hard liquor?"

"I think wine would be appropriate. White, in this case."

"Oh good, then the world is not ending."

"No, not at all, but it is getting weird."

"Pour us some wine and start talking. I'm impatient now."

"OK." I opened a bottle of nice Pinot Grigio and poured two glasses while I talked. "I've mentioned to you that my long-time wife died and afterward I moved here."

"Yes, you've told me."

I handed her a glass and sipped mine. "Before her, I was married for a short time while in college, graduate school actually. She was British and we met at a joint scientific meeting. It ended quickly and badly."

"If it was that long ago and that short of a relationship you don't need to tell me about it. We all do things in college we should not."

"Very true, and it was a mistake. I have not heard from her or seen her since it ended."

"Are you about to tell me you heard from her, or someone told you something about her?"

"Yes. I've been getting overseas calls that I've ignored. Today I answered and it was her."

"So it was a ghost from your past. What did she want?"

"She wants me to come over and help. She is apparently in trouble, something about being a suspect in a murder."

There was a long pause as Donna sipped her wine. She had a thoughtful expression rather than the mad or disappointed face I had expected. I sipped wine from my glass and waited for her response. Her next question surprised me.

"You said it ended badly. Did she end it or did you?"

"She did. Told me it wasn't working for her and I needed to go away. No other explanations, really. She was adamant, and being young and not knowing what to do, I left. The divorce was done by mail in the British system."

"Did you find out later why it happened?"

"No, nothing. I always suspected she dumped me for one of her rich classmates. But I never confirmed it as it seemed pointless."

"Then you got yourself together, finished school and met Emma. Is that accurate?"

"Close enough."

"The real question you need to ask yourself, if you have not already, is why you are the person to help her. You have to admit it sounds a bit odd."

"It is odd. But I don't know why she needs me. Other than she's in trouble and does not have anyone else to turn to."

"Lately you have been involved in murder investigations. It is likely word of that has gotten around and is probably on the internet. You need to assume she is aware of that information. That could be part of why. The rest you will find out on your own. When do you leave?"

She surprised me. "I've arranged to leave in two days. I have refundable tickets in case I decide not to go. But I don't think I'll have any answers until I get there. Now, I'd like to know how you feel about this."

"Honestly, I'm not thrilled. At the same time, if what she is saying is true, I'd be doing the same thing. You would be my first choice for helping out with a possible murder investigation, if it was me in the same situation."

"I want you to know I'm not going over there to rekindle something that fizzled more than three decades ago."

"I'm not expecting you to. But it might happen anyway. Regardless, you might also find the answers you were looking for after it ended."

"I doubt it, and it does not matter anyway."

"At least this gets you out of here and doing something exciting. How long will you be gone?"

"I am not sure, but I can't be gone more than two weeks. Between the store and Kat I've got commitments here. And I hope that includes you."

"Comparing me to a bookstore and a cat isn't helping to woo me, mister. Definitely not after telling me you are going overseas to help your ex-wife."

"That sounds bad, all of it. I wish to restate my intentions."

"Save it. You have a day or so to make up for your lapse. Then in two weeks I expect your efforts to redouble."

"I can do that. Less talking, more effort."

"That would be a good start."

Donna was more understanding than I had expected. We spent time together and she seemed fine. Then I needed to leave and she even took me to the airport. But I had one stop to make first. Millard was not home so I left a large envelope and a brief note at his house. I was going to put his Octogenarian Sleuth Force to work while I was gone.

CHAPTER FOUR

I dragged myself off the plane. No matter how many times I had flown I never liked it. I could not sleep on a plane which made the overseas flights problematic. I loaded up my phone with music and books and spent the time awake and uncomfortable. Even first class was a drag for me. My first two days after arrival was when I paid for the lack of sleep and time change.

Usually, I was on a business mission with a specific goal already set, and some downtime built in the first day to relieve the jet lag. Or I was on a vacation trip with Emma, and we always had the first day for rest, and a light second day. This trip was something different. I had no idea of the schedule or really what I was supposed to be doing. I did not enjoy the feeling. Somewhere in back of my head was the thrill of seeing her again, mitigated by the dread of seeing her.

Exiting the jet way, I stepped into the terminal. The sun was up but still early morning. Other than our international arrival flight and one other from New York, it was a quiet and empty place. I had been here twice the past ten years. Emma and I had flown in and then gone west to tour Wales one spring. Another year we flew in and went north to the Lake District. Decades ago I had been in the old version of this airport often for a couple of years, visiting my then-wife.

But no time to reminisce. I traveled light so pulled my roller along to get to passport control before the hordes descended on the understaffed border gatekeepers. I got to the big room and the lines were short. But only three gates were open of the thirty available. I chose a random line and waited while each person ahead of me averaged about six minutes each to get through the process.

Bureaucratic control was similar around the world, but the English seemed to have a special knack for inconveniencing non-citizens. It had not changed in twenty years.

Finally, it was my turn. I answered the usual banal questions. I was here for a few days, a tourist, had a return ticket, blah blah. The man took an inordinately long time paging through my American passport. He slowed at the EU resident page, then the visa pages for Russia, China, and Brazil. He even looked at the stamps for all the European and Asian countries.

"You get around a lot for American, don't you mate."

"Mostly for work. But I'm retired now, just traveling a bit for fun."

"You're young for a pensioner."

"I just look young. I have good Scottish genes." I don't think I did, but I knew it would make him mad. Mission accomplished.

"Maybe you should take the train to Scotland and stay there."

"That is what I intend. On the way I wanted to walk a bit in the Lake District ridges, then on to Inverness."

"Right. Enjoy your trip. Just don't overstay." He stamped the page harshly.

"I would not dream of it. Good day."

Then I was through and off to the train station. Conveniently they had one in the airport and one of the perks of flying into Manchester. On my way I noticed things looked different. Progress I suppose. At the station I checked my online ticket against the boards to see if anything had changed, or if there was another train to Windermere. There was, but it had two connections and two train changes. No good for my jet-lagged self so I would stay on the original ticket with only one change. I was thirty minutes early so I would just wait. I wandered around to look for a flapjack. Not the American pancake, but the English oat bar treat. Full of raisins, nuts, or whatever the local shop wanted to add to it. I desperately needed one along with a strong coffee. Unfortunately, I found neither. I settled for a hot Earl Grey tea instead. I hoped the little shop in Kendal, where I changed trains, was still in business.

The train wasn't as bad as it had been in days past. Perhaps the new initiatives moving away from the miasma of private ownership of the train lines was working. It, however was not a fast train. A lot of stops at multiple stations on the outskirts of Manchester at first. I was watching through the window rather than reading. Concrete housing mixed with commercial areas. Some stops were clean while others were not, the right of way along the track full of trash. Then small towns as the metro area gave way to the countryside with less frequent stops. Some of the villages were ancient and quaint, others were more of the twentieth century, possibly planned communities. The largest town out here was Preston. And there were sheep, lots of sheep on green grass. The land became more rolling as we lumbered north.

At Kendal I left the train to wait on the next. I had twenty-five minutes, so I checked to see if the shop was open just outside. It was, and my day got brighter. I scored a flapjack and coffee. I stood outside to consume them as the sun was out. The flapjack was nothing fancy, mostly oats, butter, brown sugar, and golden syrup. But it had a unique texture and flavor hard to replicate. Chewy yet crunchy, and a little twang from the golden syrup. I had tried to make them and knew from experience they were not easy to make. A few minutes later I was back on the next train for a short hop to the end of the line.

The Windermere stop was announced. Probably unnecessary as the train line ended there so you could not continue. The train slowed, and I rose to get my bag. I stepped off the train and onto a covered concrete area as there was no real station with old buildings, ticket counters, or covered waiting areas. I truly could not remember much about it from my previous trips, other than there was a grocery store next to it.

I went to an external board to check the bus schedule. I could have stayed on the train to Penrith, then on the bus to Keswick. But the bus ride through the Lake District from Windermere was nicer.

If I had time before the next bus, I could walk down to the lake, as Windermere was a long, thin town trailing downhill to Lake Windermere. The town and lake were on the southern edge of the several large lakes and series of high ridges that made up the Lake District. I noticed white rolling clouds were about but I didn't sense rain. The sun and clouds above the steep green hills and a distant glint of the lake made the area as picturesque as advertised. I did not have time to walk the town before the next bus. I would try to do it on the way out.

A bus ran hourly from the southern edge of the District at Windermere to the town of Keswick on the northern edge. It took about an hour to make the trip through the beautiful countryside. The environment inspired authors including William Wordsworth and many others. It was inspiring nervousness in me at the moment. Fear of what I was about to encounter mixed with the emotions of two different kinds of life I once experienced here. One with Olivia, my first wife, and the second with Emma, decades apart. And two different versions of me. Which one was going to come out on this trip?

The bus pulled up, and I texted Olivia that I was an hour away from the Keswick station. That was an exaggeration as the Keswick stop was really a patch of pavement outside a grocery store. I had given a thought that she might pick me up at Windermere and drive us across the District. That would have been an awkward hour to spend with each other, so I was glad she must have come to the same conclusion.

On the bus I now remembered why it was one of the most scenic rides I had ever taken. Not as dramatic as the Alps, but just as pretty in its tamer way. Fields and forests of various greens, backed by high barren ridges of green and brown shades. The ridges were not barren of life, but rather most human habitation. The vibrant hills sprouted patches of forest whose colors varied by the species of tree. The ridge tops were often bald and covered with various grasses and shrubs. Those accounted for the shades of greens and browns. Hidden on the ridges were the unpaved trails across the tops of most of them. Soon the ridge tops would don dustings of snow.

Long lakes like lochs filled in between ridge systems. Sometimes castle ruins appeared on the shore or on islands. Estates and farms with the ubiquitous dots of white sheep were set on the lower hills. Long piles of rock walls came down the hills to bisect the fields. Occasionally a rocky creek splashed down in a series of waterfalls. Watching all that pass by kept my mind from focusing on what was waiting at the end of the ride.

One of the clouds cut loose with a shower. The large wipers on the bus windshield began their rhythmic back and forth clicking. The rain did not detract from the ride however. The scenic countryside was still there. Nor did the sheep seem to care. Moments later the bus pulled into the Keswick stop. I stepped off and opened the umbrella. I never traveled in northern England, Scotland, or Wales without one. It kept me and my rollerbag dry, assuming there was no wind. I looked around for my ride, which I assumed would be Olivia. The few other passengers wandered off to their destinations or into the grocery store to get out of the rain.

The parking lot by the bus stop was situated between the bus drop off and the grocery. I saw a young woman in a rain jacket exit a car and approach. I assumed she was getting ready to catch the next bus.

"Mr. Wilder?" she asked, surprising me.

I deliberately took a second to look at her before answering. Perhaps twenty, average height and thin, with almost auburn hair. Definitely someone I had never met and did not know. But the accent was low Lancashire. She looked back without any expression.

"Yes," I said.

"I am Elizabeth. I'm here to fetch you."

"Hello Elizabeth. I'm ready to be fetched."

She nodded and walked back toward the car. I followed and put my bag in the trunk after she said, "the boot is open." She was in before me and I climbed in the passenger seat. Good thing she got in first as I was about to get in the wrong side. I wondered if this was a hire car or an associate of Olivia's. Elizabeth was not in a talkative mood and I decided to emulate her. Keswick was a small town, so the awkward ride could not be long. She drove east then turned south toward Castlerigg. Then into a nice housing area on a slight hill with a good view of the surrounding ridges and a bit of the lake.

Many of the houses were white tabby or siding with

grey hipped roofs. Lots of windows to catch the summer sun. High trimmed hedges encircled yards which contained gardens of colorful flowering plants. Most yards had areas with pavers or pea gravel that were equipped with chairs or benches. A few had fountains. An idyllic neighborhood and not exactly cheap. I didn't remember Olivia's parents as coming from money, so perhaps she had done well. Or it could be her husband's house but I wasn't ready to go there.

My silent driver pulled into one of the driveways and parked. We both got out and I grabbed my bag from the trunk. Elizabeth stood by the car and I wasn't sure what to say. Of course, I chose the wrong thing.

"How much do I owe you for the ride?"

"What?"

"The car hire, how much?"

"Are you daft?"

"Actually, some days I am. I assumed you were hired to carry me."

"Assumption wrong. Now, how do you know my mother?"

"What?" It was my turn to use that recently overused word.

"How do you know her?"

"Who?"

"Oh my god, you are daft. Olivia Harding, how do you know her? I'd like to know how you know her before we go in."

It finally sank in that Elizabeth was her daughter. I looked at her carefully but didn't see the resemblance from my memories of Olivia. Maybe the shape of the eyes, but that was it. Nothing else in her face, manner, or overall body type was familiar. She was waiting for an answer and growing impatient, and possibly uncomfortable with my scrutiny.

"I'm sorry, I just had no idea you were her daughter."

"That was obvious. Should I repeat my question for the third time? How does an American that does not even know her family show up here at a trying time like this?"

"I'm not exactly sure why I am here. But to answer your question, I am her husband. Very ex, obviously. That was a long time ago."

"Are you serious? I don't know you, and I've never heard of you."

"You would have to ask her. All I know is she really wanted me to come over."

"Please wait here. I'm sorry to be rude but need a word with my mother first."

This was an auspicious start to my English vacation. I stood in the light rain that had begun again and opened my umbrella. Elizabeth had stomped off and I heard a door slam. I went up to the house but did not enter. I heard a woman yelling and a softer voice answering. After some back and forth the voices went quiet. The door opened, and I turned around to face my fate.

CHAPTER FIVE

She stood there with a neutral look. I saw Elizabeth standing on the other end of the room scowling. She turned and stomped off further into the house. Olivia stepped outside under the narrow, covered stoop and closed the door. Neither of us said anything.

The woman before me was not much different other than older. However, my memory of her was competing with the view of the person before me. I remembered her as small but athletic, same as the woman before me. She was a runner and must have continued it. Straight light brown hair and grey eyes. Her hair had blonde highlights lightening it up more than I remembered. But the same face I had once cherished. A face that was lined but less than mine.

I guessed she was sizing me up the same way. How different and how old I had become compared to her memory of me? I knew I was different but not outlandishly so. She finally spoke.

"Thank you for coming, James. I'm sorry for Elizabeth's rudeness. In her defense she did not know about our previous relationship." Her voice was similar but thinner somehow.

"I gather she knew rather less than that."

"True enough. You were a topic that never came up."

"Some things don't change it seems." That got the first reaction I'd seen, a slight flinch.

"Fair enough. I have kept that part of my past from my family. I never expected it to be brought up."

"Yet now it has. Picking me up seems a rather unkind chore to send her on. Does she get paid to drive your ex-husbands from the bus stop?

"Just the ones that are alive."

"Brutal, but I suppose honest enough."

"I would have sent her brother, Ian, but he isn't home. I was tied up with the police."

"Olivia, what am I doing here?"

"As I told you, I need help. There has been a death, most likely a murder. I'm a suspect."

"Did you do it?"

"Forthright as ever. No, I did not."

I was not always a good judge of character. But my gut

usually indicated whether or not I was hearing the truth. In this case, I detected no falsehood.

"I believe you."

"You believe me? Just like that?"

"Yes."

"Does that make you wise or foolish?"

"Yes."

She finally let a thin smile appear. "That attitude has not changed."

"Where am I staying?"

"The Clareridge Inn just down the street. It is within walking distance. They also have bikes for hire if you want to go into Keswick. Or it is close enough to walk, but you are American. Do you need a car for the half-mile journey?"

"No thanks, I'll walk when sunny and bike when not windy. If its rainy and windy, I'll stay inside and sip tea."

"That is very British of you."

"Well, I studied the lifestyle since I once considered becoming a citizen. But soon enough I had no reason to."

"Let's not get into this now. You must be tired. I'll take you to your lodging. Or Elizabeth can drive you."

"No thanks, I'd rather walk."

"Follow this lane down the hill. At the road turn right and the Inn is on the right. Can't miss it."

"Are we going to talk later?"

"I'll walk to the Inn and we can supper there."

"Without Elizabeth?"

"Definitely without Elizabeth. I'll be spending the rest of the afternoon dealing with her."

"Good luck." I left with my rollerbag tagging noisily

behind me. The rain had ceased and some sun threatened to beam past the clouds. I liked the sights and smells of the English countryside after a shower. Other than the annoying bag it was near perfect. I finally picked it up and carried it as the pavers seemed endless. At the bottom of the hill and the main road, a concrete sidewalk appeared, and I put it down again. Now there was only a crack every three feet to make a sound and annoy me. Moments later I was at the Clareridge and signed in. Before going up I perused the downstairs and looked out the back. To satisfy my curiosity and maybe check for escape routes.

It was a much larger version of the homes I had just left. Three stories of white walls with a grey roof and extensive gardens on both sides and the back. I counted ten rooms upstairs. On the ground level was a small lobby, large common room with fireplace and books, and a combination dining area and bar. Glass doors led to the rear with a car park. There was room for ten narrow cars in pea gravel immediately outside. A gate and path past that to the gardens that went uphill. I would visit that later. I walked up to my room and unpacked my small bag.

That done, I showered to remove what I always thought of as the oily airplane grime. I felt better with only a twinge of jet lag. Rather than take a nap I dressed and went down to the bar. An attendant took my order and brought me a hot tea kettle with a nice loose-leaf house blend. I poured the first cup and a moment later tasted it. Excellent. Now to business.

I was in Keswick. A beautiful town in a wonderful setting. I was here at the request of my wife from ages ago I had not heard from since. Now I had met her daughter who knew nothing about me. Apparently, she had a brother that I assumed also knew nothing of me. There was no mention of the father and husband yet. Olivia lived in a very nice house. I met Olivia and had a brief chat. She was suspected in a death. She needed help with the situation. OK, those were the facts.

Now the difficult part—how did I feel about all this? I needed to go through it now before Olivia came down. That way I would begin dealing with all the emotional stuff now, then when she arrived I could be professional and determine how to help her. If I even could.

Olivia had a family. Based on what I guessed the ages were of her children, she must have started a family about five years after our breakup. Approximately the same time I was marrying Emma. She lived in a nice house in a nice area.

Did I need to know any details about the husband or children? No, not unless they were involved in the death or for providing an alibi if needed. Should I divulge anything about my family or life? Probably unnecessary. I would keep it out of any discussions since it was irrelevant. Olivia likely would not ask so that should be easy.

I was now finished with my second cup of tea and the pot was cooling. I felt I had my emotions dealt with for the moment. Keep it professional and work the problem; investigate the case and go home. That should be easy. Then why was I so nervous about seeing Olivia at supper? We had once spent a week hiking between Keswick and Windermere. Ascending the ridges and walking during the day, then dropping back down to stay at cheap hostels or a bed and breakfast each evening. We had a great time, maybe the best of our brief stint together. We talked of someday moving to Keswick once we were rich and famous. Now we were both back in Keswick after very different paths in life. These memories and feelings were what I needed to deal with and put away before she arrived.

Olivia texted me she was on her way. I went to the dining area and picked out a table. It was the most private one in the open dining area. It was early, and I knew from checking in that several rooms were empty, so we should be able to chat without too much problem. The server came out and I ordered a glass of wine. I would rather have had iced tea, but I was a few thousand miles away from that option. Olivia strode in wearing navy and white. I remembered that was a favorite combination of hers. It still looked good on her, which was a thought best left unsaid.

I stood to welcome her. She surprised me by stepping up and giving me a brief hug. As we stepped back she said, "Good evening Dr. Wilder."

"And good evening to you, Dr.?" I left the question hanging as I did not know what last name she used.

"Dr. Stewart is my official name," she said. "Although outside of the profession I still go by Harding."

"Good evening Dr. Stewart. Would you like a glass of wine?"

"Yes, whatever you are having."

I caught the server's attention and ordered another glass, along with dinner. We sat quietly and looked at each other. Somehow it was not uncomfortable. There was a time we knew each other so well we didn't need to talk, and maybe we still did. Her wine delivered, she sipped it then broke the silence.

"I suppose we should catch up a bit. Is that appropriate, do you think?"

"Earlier I thought about it and decided it was not. But now after further consideration I don't see how we can't. I need to get to know you and your situation."

"Sensible. I'll go first with the questions. Do you have a family?"

"Yes, but my wife died relatively recently. Just before we could take early retirement together. Our son is in northern California. He is doing well, married, and no children. They try to get back for one holiday a year or I go out to visit annually. How about your family?"

"You've met Elizabeth, my daughter. She is a handful but a nice person somewhere under that attitude. My son Ian is at the university in Glasgow."

"As I remember, you went to university in Edinburgh."

"I did. Elizabeth chose Manchester."

"Oh, so Keswick is in between. That is convenient."

"It can be. Ian does not visit very often anymore."

"Well, at his age he probably has friends and a significant other in Glasgow. Living his life as a college student."

"That would be one explanation."

"Elizabeth must take after her father as she does not resemble you."

"That is true. Somewhat the same with Ian, although he did get my eye color. But enough of that. Tell me about your career." I noticed she had so far avoided mention of her husband.

"What career? I gave that up completely."

"I thought you were the global expert on several topics."

"Topics of not much notice or importance. When I disappeared, there wasn't even a ripple. Although a few contemptible consultants probably made some money."

"Does that bother you?"

"At the very beginning. Then I realized it was nothing personal. Once you leave the corporate world you lose all value, which was little enough to begin with. CEOs get celebrated, everyone gets forgotten the day you no longer make them money. Same with academia. For my part, I don't miss either and rarely even consider my previous work."

"You spent time working in both areas?"

"I bounced back and forth between academic positions and private industry. Even spent a few years with the federal government."

"You always seemed to be looking for something even in our old days."

"I was. I was under the mistaken assumption that out there was a great place I would find to work and build a career. But I soon found that private industry was only interested in the monthly profit-loss sheet, at the cost of everything and everyone else. The universities were starved by state legislatures, so they became money hungry. Loss of academic integrity soon followed as professors chased only money. Both industry and academics became filled with venal humans."

"I bet your idealism did not endear you to your colleagues."

"At first there were more of us than them. Now there is almost nothing there but them. You can see the result. A sharp rise in corporate and academic cheating. Corporations break rules and lie while researchers falsify research projects to get grants."

"I have noticed that, even here."

"What about your career?"

"After graduate school, I was always on the industry side even with my scientific background. Early on there was always a place for a highly qualified technical woman willing to take low pay. That was me. After a few years I found myself doing more business things. It was the only way to get promoted and compete for salary increases. I ended up out of the technical side completely and in business management exclusively."

"Where you got to supervise people."

"Yes, and it was ghastly. Two people, then ten, twenty, fifty. Mostly what I did was manage those people's lives to get them to be productive for the company."

"You said it as if it was past tense."

"It is past. Last year the company I had been so loyal to made me redundant."

"What happened?"

"Nineteen of us senior staff, at the director or upper manager level, were let off. We found out later the company had secretly bought our biggest rival. Part of the deal was our company would take on many of their senior people. So, out we went and the next day in they came."

"The ones they kept and replaced your people with—most were white males?"

"Of course."

"That must sting."

"It did, a lot. I was out of sorts for weeks."

"I remember how much you liked your daily planner and keeping up with details."

"It got worse as I got older and took on more responsibility. When let go I nearly could not function. But after several weeks, I realized it was an opportunity. I could get my life back. Regain what I had ignored and suppressed for many years."

"What does that look like?"

"It is still ongoing. But so far, it has been my inadequate attempt to spend more time with my children. Gardening as the weather allows. Little things that I seem to have missed along my career path."

"Anyone buried in those gardens?"

"I'll get around to that later."

"Tell me what my job is."

"Since I did not do it, I'd like you to find enough answers so there are no questions about my innocence. Just as important, protect my children from any of this."

"I'll do what I can."

CHAPTER SIX

Our food arrived and we took another pause. I thought that talking to her was easy, much too easy. It was as if we picked up, not where we left off, but before then when we were still good.

"Now on to current matters. Why am I here?"

"For reasons. They are not very good, however."

"Tell me anyway."

"I need someone to help me get through the next few days. Someone logical without any ties to my current life."

"Surely you have friends that could assist."

"I really don't. And my children are much too close to all this to help."

I drew back to remember the old Olivia. She had family, sisters, she was close to. Work colleagues she went to bars with after work. But I only remember her having one close friend in her life. Not enough to sustain through decades of moving, marrying, and having children. I suspect she really did not have anyone close to her anymore.

"What are you thinking about?" she asked.

"I was trying to remember your family and friends. I did not come up with much."

"Over the years I've grown apart from my close family. I never really carried many friends, and those I had are long since out of my life. There, those are the bad reasons I called you."

"I see you are not wearing a wedding ring. There is no husband to help you either."

"That is the rather sticky part. I am a person of interest in his death."

"Ah, now we get to the good part. Even if you had family or close friends they would not be of much use, since they would be caught up in whatever this is."

"True enough. And why I need you more than them now. That is all this is about."

"On the surface at least. I suspect there is more going on, but I'll let things play out for a time."

"What do you suspect?"

"I have no idea yet. But there is always something else going on. Now for the important question—did you kill him?"

"No, I did not."

"Issue solved, you don't need me. Now I can get on with a vacation in the Lake District."

"It's not that simple. Campbell was not a very nice person. There are complications from his actions while alive, and from his death."

"Sounds like you need to apologize."

"Why should I apologize to you?"

"Not me. You need to apologize to your children for keeping a bad man around as their father."

"It's not that easy."

"It needs to be. I noticed how unhappy Elizabeth seems."

"She hates you. And me, of course."

"But she doesn't even know me. That means she's equating me to your husband. Probably thinks you are dragging another bad man into her life."

"How dare you make implications about me, about my marriage, or my children's happiness."

"It is what I am here to do. Investigate anything and everything and eventually clear you of wrongdoing if you are innocent. No reason to take my questions and implications personally."

"If I'm innocent?" I thought it interesting that is what she took as the important part of what I said.

"Yes, if. I doubt you did anything. But I must begin with that as everyone is a suspect until proven otherwise."

"I thought that would be your null hypothesis. That I was innocent and did not kill anyone."

"You are correct, the null hypothesis is valid for a scientific experiment. This will be anything but a controlled experiment. You need to know it will get messy, and I'll get into things in your life and business you will wish I had not. Or I can start my vacation now. Your call."

She leaned back in thought. I was on the verge of extracting myself from this quagmire. The silence stretched on as we both drank our wine. She was either playing me or really considering her options. I realized I knew so little about her that I could not tell which.

"Very well. It is in my best interest that you stay and investigate my husband's death. I accept there will be consequences to your work that I may not like. I only ask you keep my children out of this."

"I can't do that. They are an intrinsic part of your life and what is going on in it, as well as your late husband. At their age, they are necessary for background character, and may even be witnesses or suspects."

Now she was really mad, uncomfortable, or both. "No I can't have that, it won't happen. I'll give you money for your flight and hotel room tomorrow. Enjoy your vacation." She got up and left.

Perhaps I had pushed her too far. Or there was a deep dark family secret she had to keep hidden at all costs. Or something worse, if she suspected one of them was involved in the death. But it was all speculation on my part as I didn't have much to go on. What I had not told Olivia was my investigation had begun even before I got on the plane. Nothing specific, it was more about how to goad her answers and set up future questions. Then I had begun my initial analysis after meeting Elizabeth, and tonight was just the beginning of my efforts.

My bet was that in the morning Olivia would show up with the money to call my bluff. Then she would ask me to stay on, after having the evening to plan how to keep me out of certain parts of her personal life, or those of her children. I had already met Elizabeth, but she would likely be sent back to the university. I doubted I would ever meet her son.

Since we had finished dinner, I took my wine and walked out back to the garden. There were things I both liked and disliked about England, which was true of every place I had ever been. But one thing I liked were the gardens. A lot of people were dedicated to the thoughtful and long-term pursuit of a great garden. It was something I truly appreciated. My time there was well spent as I went over our recent conversation. Then back to my room to write a few notes and try to sleep, despite the jet lag threatening to keep me awake.

My English breakfast, eaten late as I caught up on sleep, was wonderful. English bacon, eggs, tomatoes, beans, bread and pastries, and great tea. This was in the same category of good as their gardens. As expected, I saw Olivia enter the dining room. She looked weary, and I felt a slight pang of compassion.

"Good morning, Olivia. How was your evening?"

"Not great. I think our conversation, on top of everything else happening, left me quite out of sorts. My appearance is a testament to my lack of sleep."

"Did you send Elizabeth away?"

"I tried to. She absolutely refused. How did you know?"

"Part of my analysis is to anticipate people's reaction to certain types of stimulus."

"Are you treating me like an experimental animal?"

"No, more like a hostile witness. Are you paying me off

and sending me on vacation? Or have you had time to come up with a plan to keep me away from your secrets?"

"I think I have my secrets secured."

"Then the game is on, and I will expose them. But I will not do anything merely to either shame or antagonize you, I promise. There may be times you think so, but I have no lingering animosity. The way I see it, my best outcome is to quickly clear you and your family of any wrongdoing. But that means I must know more about you than you will be comfortable with. I need to know much more than those who are investigating you for this to work. Your strategies to keep secrets may be good, but my job is to drag them out, so you can make them stronger."

"That is an interesting strategy. I suppose I don't care as long as you can make this go away."

"Would you like some breakfast? Mine was excellent. I believe food and tea would do you good."

"I would actually. How can you be so chipper after your travels? It is an annoying trait."

"I think it is likely my delight in anticipation of antago-nizing you."

"I know you are teasing. I suppose I deserve it after teasing you last night. But if you keep it up before I get my tea I might just throttle you."

"Throttle on, Olivia. But I will give you peace until after tea. Then I have a few hundred questions to begin asking you."

"I opened this doorway to hell, didn't I?"

"You do get the privilege of deciding where the inquisition takes place."

"I'll do it after tea. Time for you to stop talking."

I peacefully sipped my tea and contemplated having a scone. It was my biggest decision of the morning. I studied Olivia's face as she scrolled through her phone, then devoured two cups of tea and a breakfast. Not for the first time on this trip, I wondered who she was and, by proxy, who I was to be sitting here with her. My first thought was that I was here to ferret out a death and suspects, if needed. It seemed to be what I did recently.

CHAPTER SEVEN

Olivia finally finished her breakfast and tea without speaking. I didn't mind at all.

"I still don't know how you do it," she said.

"What is that?"

"Embrace the silence. You are so comfortable with not speaking. Most people I know can't stop talking for thirty seconds."

"You should get to know different people. Hanging with extroverts all the time will make you haggard."

"You not talking makes people want to talk to you. You

listen, and they want to talk more. It's how you find out more than most people."

"It is one strategy to get information. In my case it comes naturally, so I might as well make use of it."

"What do you want to know?"

"This sounds flippant, but I want to know everything since at least a week before the death occurred."

"I think we need to go to my house. I'd rather not the whole Inn hear everything. There are also several items you need to read."

"Great, I'll get my rain jacket. I assume you walked."

"I did."

"Let's walk back together and we can begin."

Walking with Olivia past the gardens along the way, near Keswick of all places, was a surreal experience. If we had held hands I would have been transported back thirty-five years. But this was now, so no hand-holding, just questions about a dead man. The times they were indeed changing.

"Olivia, when was your husband killed?"

"He was found dead more than a week ago."

"Why are you a suspect?"

"I suppose because I am his wife, but we had a difficult history in recent years. Also because he was found not far away at the bottom of a cliff on one of the high trails. No witnesses, so the police seem to be focusing on me."

"Do you have a lawyer?"

"Of course. I have a solicitor and he has a barrister ready to go if the legal case proceeds."

"What does he or she say about whether you are a prime suspect?"

"He is not sure yet. He believes that if they had a strong case, anything really, I'd already be in custody. But he's puzzled I'm a suspect at all. Normally the police would not keep after me with such a weak case. Rather, they would quietly investigate and arrest me if evidence supported their case. Continuing to question me and keep me as a person of interest is apparently unusual."

"I don't know the criminal system here so I can't speculate. So he was found dead, and they keep questioning you for no apparent purpose."

"Correct."

"What were the circumstances of his death?"

"I can give you more details of his injuries and cause of death when we get to the house as its in the preliminary report. A group of hikers one morning spotted what they thought was a body below a cliff. One of them climbed down and confirmed. They called it in and the local police went out and processed the scene."

"Then they came to question you?"

"No, first they came to tell me Campbell was dead. It was several days later before the questioning began. I called you after the third session. They've been here twice since then."

"That does sound odd, five sessions in a few days. They must be fishing for something. Or they want to badger you into a confession. But why could it not have been an accident?"

"That is what both me and my solicitor have been trying to sort out."

"I remember occasional hiking deaths in the District over the years, but not any murders."

"Only a few instances of men killing their wives, or the mass shooter incident. It is normally a civil place."

The conversation paused as we arrived at Olivia's house. We went in and soon saw Elizabeth in the kitchen. She gave us both a withering stare. The tirade quickly began without any greetings.

"Why didn't you ever tell me about him?" Elizabeth asked Olivia. Apparently I was not going to be part of the conversation, other than as an object. My presence was ignored.

"It was never important, so it didn't come up," Olivia answered.

"Didn't want me to know about another of your stupid mistakes, is more like it."

"It did not concern you. My mistakes are my own, especially those made years before your conception. The statute of limitations expired long since."

Elizabeth was searching for a rebuttal but didn't come up with anything. She resorted to stomping off to somewhere else in the house. I felt the brief exchange was for my benefit, so Elizabeth could show she was still outraged.

"She does stomping well," I said. "Family trait?"

"Better than talking each other to death like the Americans."

"Agreed. I will also take up stomping. It could become more popular than cricket."

"Any sport in America is more popular than cricket."

"How many cricket games have you, as a British citizen, watched and enjoyed?"

"Please. I'd rather take a winter dip in the North Sea than watch that tripe."

"I knew it. The British hate it but foist it on the colonies as torture."

"They are not colonies anymore. Rather, members of the Commonwealth."

"You are right, that sounds better than colonies. Then it doesn't imply the English were colonizers."

"Whatever. Do you want tea before reading up on the documents?"

"Sure, whatever you are having."

Olivia put on the kettle and went to get the papers. I got a glimpse of Elizabeth in the hallway but she didn't return to the kitchen. The dining and living rooms were adjacent so I went to the living area to look at photographs. There were not many, and I saw none of anyone that might be Olivia's husband. Just a few of Elizabeth and a boy that must have been Ian. Not much resemblance to Olivia as she'd said, other than the grey eyes. Olivia returned with a slim folder and we sat at the dining table. We poured water over tea leaves in the cup strainer before speaking. Olivia slid the folder over to me.

I opened it to two documents, which I skimmed through. Then I reread both slowly. The first was a summary of findings containing the bare facts and no notes. The second was longer with details and notes.

I learned the basic details of Campbell Stewart's life and death from the first document. His age, size, physical description, and place of birth. About my age but a large man. Whether muscle or excess flesh I had no way of knowing, nor could I corroborate since there were no photos. The place of death and approximate time of death.

The second, longer document gave more typed details.

A narrative about the group that found him, recovery efforts, and more details on the physical body. It was not a full autopsy report, but did recite the cause of death was blunt-force trauma to the head, several broken bones and contusions. There was internal organ damage. It indicated death from a probable fall, and that he was alive when he fell. I knew that was from the types of bruises, which only occurred if there was blood pressure. A dead body with no blood pressure can't bruise. Two notable bruises were a linear one across the forearm and another across the knee. If he had struck a sharp edge on a rock shelf, that would have done it. The toxicology testing showed no drugs or chemicals other than alcohol. But it was low, and he was not drunk. Probably residual from drinks at dinner.

My tea was done and I looked up to see Olivia watching me.

"Olivia, other than this man, Campbell, being dead, I don't see anything here indicating murder or wrongful death."

"I did not either. My solicitor said it may be intentional. The police could be declining to release anything to indicate murder. Part of a strategy to surprise me if they press any charges."

"Do you mind if I look around the house?"

"Why, what are you looking for?"

"I don't know. I suppose to get a feel for the family. But I'd like to wander through the rooms and then do the same outside."

"I really don't believe that will help. But go ahead. I'll let Elizabeth know as she may wish to leave."

"Makes sense. I'll start in these three rooms anyway."

After Olivia left I heard words exchanged in the back of the house and Elizabeth stomped by and left through the door with a huff. She was making me glad I didn't have a daughter. But then having her father recently dead and her mom's ex in the house could not have been pleasant.

I opened doors as I walked around. There were no men's jackets, gloves, boots or hats in the closets. In fact, no men's clothes at all in the bedrooms. Other than what must have been Ian's room. I also saw no tools or outdoor gear that was noticeably male. I wondered if Olivia had already de-spoused the house. I found a nice garden room to the rear of the house. Lots of glass and comfortable-looking chairs. Then there was a hallway that had stairs. I continued down and found several bedrooms, one of which was converted to an office. I could immediately tell it was Olivia's.

I opened a door and found Elizabeth's bedroom. Standing there I took in the sight but did not go inside. I saw nothing but what might be expected of a young college student. Another door and I found Ian's room. A male version of Elizabeth's but more sparsely furnished. The back bedroom was Olivia's room and had a large attached bath. I walked into the room then the bath. The medicine cabinet nor any of the storage shelves or linen closet contained anything that was noticeably male. Had I not known she was married, I never would have guessed she was, based on what the house told me.

I heard Olivia moving around upstairs. Going up I found two bedrooms and a bath. One of the rooms had quite a few books and the other was mostly storage. Olivia was in that room going through boxes. I went in to see if any men's items were obvious, but there was nothing.

"Finding what you are looking for?" she asked.

"No, nothing much. I'm going out to the gardens. Is there a storage shed out there?"

"Yes, and it is unlocked."

I went down and out the back door. The gardens appeared as if they had been let go for a time but were recently being tended. That matched Olivia's story. The shed was nothing more than outdoor storage and garden implements. Whatever I was looking for regarding Campbell's presence was not in the house or on the property. Turning left I went around the side of the house. The area was still grown up but there was a bench under a heavy vine. Elizabeth was sitting and glaring at me.

"Why are you really here?" she asked.

"I believe my primary role is to torment Olivia's daughter. I seem to be successful."

She continued with the death stare. Somehow I lived.

"Why are you creeping around?"

"I'm trying to get a feel for who Campbell Stewart was."

"Don't bother. He's dead." I refrained from reacting, but her response told me a lot.

"I know, but to investigate I need an understanding of who he was, what he did and why. That includes his interaction with his family."

"I have nothing to say about that." She rose and moved toward the house.

"Elizabeth?" She stopped and turned, but did not respond. "Spare the grass. Stomping hurts it."

I got another huff as she continued stomping away.

Then she walked normally after I said in a high-pitched voice, "we hurts, we hurts." I heard her say something like "weird American" as she went into the house.

I sat on the bench a moment, fully realizing there was nothing of Campbell in this place. I had not accomplished anything other than mimicking hurt grass. My turn to sigh as I got up and went inside. Elizabeth was having a tough time and I would not add to that on purpose. I'd try humor to defuse her. In the kitchen, Olivia motioned for me to sit with her at the table.

"I took the liberty of heating more water," she said. "Another cup of tea?"

"Yes, thanks."

"Any thoughts so far?"

"I have not conducted many murder investigations, but this is the slowest and strangest one I have done."

"That sounds unpromising."

"No matter how I tried, I could not get a sense of Campbell in this place. Not that it matters that much, but I thought it would have been a starting point for my investigation."

"You will have to try something different."

"Is there a course titled 'Obviousity' at the British universities these days?"

"Perhaps. Would you like to stay for lunch or go out?"

"The weather is promising so I would like to go to Keswick. I need to pick up things I'll be needing that I didn't bring."

"I'll leave you to it unless I can drop you there."

"No thanks, I'll bike from the Inn."

Keswick was a scenic town and easily walkable. A lot of the older buildings and houses had stone walls and grey roofs. There were also a lot of white walls in town. Much of the newer construction had walls of white siding, while some of the older buildings were white-washed to give the stone a light color.

The retail shops were stocked to maximize products for customers in regard to the town's proximity to the Lake District. Boating and hiking were the main pursuits, with biking coming in a close third. Although many tourists came just to see the scenery, walk about, shop, and depart without engaging in any outdoor activities.

I biked into the town center to shop. I had the basics in the small bag I had brought, but I needed sturdier and more specific items for my expected traipsing about. Knowing Keswick had everything I would need once I got here was the reason I traveled here with a small bag. Everything I bought I would use on the Pine Mountain hikes once home.

The first items to find were good boots and socks. Then a proper rain jacket and a light wool sweater. Also, a light-weight scarf and a wool baseball-style cap. I needed to buy a second bag as well to take the new purchases back with me. All the items to be bought were needed for the ridge walks. Experience had taught me to be prepared even this early in the fall. A sunny warm day could turn foggy, or more often into a gale with sleet in less than an hour. On the high ridge with no cover it was dangerous to get caught unprepared.

The socks were easy to find once I found a shop selling the Falke brand. The boots took longer as I was looking for a specific type and weight. The real problem was finding a pair with plenty of cushion. Plenty of styles had that but were more of a trail shoe and not leather or waterproof. I finally found some that would work. The rest of the items were quickly found with all the stores selling similar cloth-ing. One shop I bought from offered to deliver my pack-ages back to the Inn. Even the packages bought elsewhere. I gladly accepted and brought everything back to them. I tipped the delivery driver as well as it saved me from putting everything on the bike, then worrying about the packages as I parked and explored more of the town and lakefront.

I was the American with the worst accent in town, but everyone was nice. They were used to tourists from all over, and as long as I was polite the locals would accept me. People in Keswick had always been friendly when I was there. I was enjoying myself, and it must have been evident. During my shopping, I noticed a younger man who seemed to be habiting the same shops I was. Not unusual, as tourists usually made the same rounds where they knew to get the good stuff.

My shopping had a dark side. My ridge hikes, at least one of them, would be to the place where the body was found. I would go by myself as I didn't want any outside influence. I needed to go on a day with good weather, and possibly a second time in the evening around when the coroner said death occurred. It was the only way to understand the environment and possibly determine whether it was an accident or if it was murder.

But for now, I rode to the waterfront to enjoy the wide view of the lake with mountains in every direction, giving the water plenty of images to reflect. The sky was brilliant blue with puffy white clouds tinged with grey, also reflecting in the water. There were lots of wooden rowboats and a few sailboats lined up on the waterfront and docks and three sailboats on the lake tacking away from where I stood with my bike. Just across a short piece of water was an island with a dock and large stone building. It was quite a swatch of real estate. I just needed a few more million in my bank account and a knighthood to get one just like it. I vaguely remembered it as Derwent Island.

There was a story about the original owner who developed it a couple of hundred years ago, but I could not recall the details.

A long wooden boat came slicing through the water toward the docks. The Derwentwater Ferry was arriving. It taxied hikers and tourists around the lake to a few destinations. I intended to take it to get some photos and take a hike on the high ridge opposite of town. But not today as I wasn't prepared for an extended hike. If a few of those clouds got together on top of where I was, it would get most unpleasant. But now I had the clothes to outfit myself, so I would be back.

I watched a few people get off the boat. They reminded me of something I needed to do. I was not sure how to do it in this country, but there must be a way. And Olivia should be able to help. If Campbell was murdered, whoever did it had to arrive in Keswick to do so. If by car, I probably could not get access to all cameras around the area, nor did I have any way to sift through that mass of information. But if they arrived by bus or train, and I could arrange access, then I could review those tapes or digital feeds for potential suspects.

I pedaled back to the Inn. My packages from the day's shopping had already been delivered. I dined solo and made plans via text to see Olivia late afternoon the next day. She seemed surprised we were not meeting in the morning, but I didn't tell her what I was doing. The next morning, I dressed appropriately and caught a bus for a ridge hike. I knew from the report where to go. The bus ride, as always, was an easy way to get around the District.

At the designated stop, I got off and began the steep

hike up the ridge. The initial steepness dissuaded a lot of people who ended up missing out on easy hikes and incredible views once at the top. Then it was easy to walk the ridge to the next bus stop, descend, and ride home.

The view from the top was lovely. In the distance was a green valley and glimpses of a blue lake. A town was partially visible nestled on one portion of the lakeshore. The foreground was rock and a slight green from lichen. The other side was more bleak, a high valley only a hundred or so feet below the ridge on which I was standing. More browns and greys, with patches of less vibrant green. What grew up here was tormented by the wind and winter weather. A small pond, what the English called a tarn was toward the far end, its surface ruffled by the wind. The other side of the narrow valley was a rocky ridge. Above, the sky was perhaps a third brilliant blue, the rest heavily punctuated by billowy white and grey clouds moving at a fast clip. The sun shadows followed along the ground accordingly. Although the wind was brisk, it was not uncomfortable. But I knew the wind could double at any time and sleet could appear, driven nearly sideways by the gusts. Anyone hiking had best be prepared for the fast changes.

The trail followed a bench that narrowed and rose higher. Soon the trail was little more than a narrow ridge of rock with drops on both sides. Falling off to the green valley side was survivable. Scrapes and bruises likely unless you banged your head on some of the boulders protruding through the grass and shrubs. The other side, however, looked more lethal. Steeper and nothing but rock to break your fall the first thirty feet, then a narrow rock ledge over a sheer drop to the valley floor. If you somehow survived the first section and stopped on the ledge, you might survive. But the second, longer drop would assuredly kill you. The bottom beyond that drop is where Campbell's body was found. Hikers the next day saw his jacket, a distinct green and bright yellow design.

Mentally, I brought up the report of Campbell's death. Now I saw why there were multiple contusions, several broken bones, a fractured skull, internal bleeding and organ damage. The cliff was high and peppered with rocks below, so he must have died on impact. No signs of foul play, such as strangulation or defensive cuts on the body. He fell and died. The only question was whether he fell by accident or was pushed. He could have jumped, but I thought that was the least likely scenario.

His phone was missing. A search of the area had not found it, nor had it pinged anywhere. That was odd since he had either not brought it or someone had taken it from him before the fall. I did not think anyone would have had the time or ability to go down and remove it from the body. But it could have happened. But no broken bits from the phone body or screen were found in the clothing or nearby rocks. Maybe it was lodged up high somewhere in the cliff, but I had no intention of climbing and searching.

I did want to see the bottom, so I backtracked several hundred yards. Then I went off the trail where it was less steep and angled toward the cliff bottom. It was still rough going with the rocks but doable with care. It took me twenty minutes to get to the bottom of the cliff. Going up was not going to be pleasant. I looked around but saw nothing unusual. There could have been blood stains on two rocks, but if so, they were faded to a thin black coating. Looking up, I estimated the narrow ledge was about thirty feet from the top, then another seventy feet from the ledge to where I stood at the bottom. I climbed back up, and it was as unpleasant as I had expected.

Something not mentioned in the report was Campbell's car. Where was it found, or did he arrive in Keswick another way? That reminded me I needed to get Olivia to help me with accessing cameras at the bus and train stops.

I caught a bus after hiking from the ridge down to the road since it was a common practice in the Lake District. If you had a cheap place to stay and rode the bus to various hikes, it was a great and inexpensive vacation in a beautiful setting. I had once done it with Olivia. But I had never imagined so many years later I'd be hiking alone to see where Olivia's husband died.

I changed at the Inn and walked to Olivia's house. She had invited me to dinner. I didn't know whether it would be contentious or peaceful. It could depend on whether Elizabeth was present. I knew Olivia did not want me talking to her daughter, but at some point I needed to question her about her father. I did not have long to wait. As I approached the house, Elizabeth met me on the front walk. She still didn't look happy, but she wasn't seething with anger anymore.

"On your last visit you said you were trying to get an idea of the man who lived here," she said.

"That's right. But there wasn't anything here to find."

"That's because he didn't live here. I don't suppose mum volunteered that information."

"No, she did not. I basically have to treat her as a hostile witness."

"Oh, I like that. I believe I'll use it."

"Please do. But I hope sometime you and your mom work things out."

"Maybe. But she has other major sins besides not telling you everything."

"We all do." She began to walk away. "Elizabeth?" I asked, and she stopped and turned. "Thanks for telling me." She nodded and continued on to the house. Olivia was still keeping her dumb secrets, but at least Elizabeth could now have a two-sentence conversation with me without stomping away. Even if it was only to make Olivia look bad.

"What was that about?" Olivia asked as she met me at the door.

"Something we can talk about after dinner."

"Come in and have some wine. Dinner is ready."

"Hope you didn't go to too much trouble cooking."

"I did not, in fact, go to any trouble. We are having take-away from the Asian place in Keswick."

"Did I mention I'm allergic to Asian food?" Olivia froze and just looked at me. I held her gaze, then I broke. "Just kidding, Asian food is fine," I said with a smile.

"Sod off and forage for yourself," she muttered, but she was smiling too.

The food was a variety of items, including spring rolls, satay chicken, tempura shrimp, ginger fried rice, kung po beef and orange chicken. It was enough for eight people. Olivia must have been hungry when ordering. Elizabeth did not show up for food, so we ate for a few minutes and then put the rest in the refrigerator.

"Are you going to tell me what you've been doing, or is it a secret?" Olivia asked.

"My shopping in Keswick was mostly for hiking purposes. With my new outfit I went hiking."

"Sprinkling vacation pursuits in with your efforts to exonerate me?"

"I guess it was both. I wanted to see where your husband died."

"What did you discover?"

"He had good taste in choosing where to die. Very scenic."

"Campbell liked that path. I did not, but he insisted on taking us there at least twice a year when the kids were younger. When I was working or traveling, he took them on his own. And that wasn't a nice thing to say."

"I have a habit of saying things like that when I'm being played. When you were speaking of secrets, just know I don't have any that I'm keeping. Unlike you."

"What do you mean?"

"The chat I had before dinner with Elizabeth. She confirmed my observations that your husband did not live here." Olivia looked neither surprised nor contrite. I was not surprised in her lack of reaction. "Where did he live?"

"Macclesfield. We have a house there. This house was the summer and getaway house."

"Yet you and apparently your children have been living here instead. Would you like to tell me why?"

"We have been living apart for more than two years. Macclesfield is closer to his business interests. I remained here as we needed some distance."

"Was there a reason you did not tell me? You must have thought it was funny watching me waste time figuring out Campbell did not live in this house."

"It was not that. I'm not ready to talk about the… separation. Especially not to a previous ex-husband."

"You might be brought up on murder charges. Maybe you should get ready."

"You seem angry."

"Being around you and your idiotic machinations and omissions does that. You are either playing silly games or want to go to jail. Either way, I am of no use to you."

"You have a right to be mad. But my reasons are my own. And I can't tell you."

"Fine. I'll find out anyway. As I told you before, your secrets pertaining to your marriage to Campbell are fair game. If you don't tell me, I'll pry them from someone else. You know I won't let go until I know everything I need to."

She did not say anything. She knew she was wrong, but something was keeping her from talking about her issues with Campbell. Time to change tactics.

"Olivia, I would like to visit the Macclesfield house."

"Why, what do you need from there?"

"I don't know. That is why I'd like to go. I need to see the house, the grounds. More importantly, his study or office. I need to know more about who he was and what he did."

"I really don't think it necessary. The police have

already been through the house and his study. But I will take you because I know you won't let it go."

"Thanks. Have you been there since his death?"

"No, I have not. It is close to three hours drive. I'll be taking a bag as we'll be staying overnight."

"I'll do the same. Will you pick me up at the Inn in the morning?"

"I'll be over at half past eight."

I wondered about Olivia's reaction, or perhaps lack of reaction. She seemed incurious about Campbell's personal space and what was in it. It seemed she had written him off and no longer cared to know much about him or what happened. Strange since she was supposedly being looked at as a suspect in his death. But she was hiding something she felt was more important than being a murder suspect.

Since we were finished with dinner, I took my leave and walked back to the Inn. It was a beautiful evening and being outside and near the gardens helped to relieve my frustrations.

The morning drive down to Macclesfield was scenic and we passed lots of interesting places. But Olivia was quiet and in her own thoughts as she drove. I was not going to complain as it gave me an opportunity to view the green hills and steep streams we passed. And lots of sheep.

Visiting England and Ireland I rarely drove. I sat on what I considered the wrong side of the car and was impressed as Olivia drove, using her left hand to shift, pull the parking brake when stopped on an incline, and drive without a second thought. I could drive perfectly well in America, but there was no way I could do the British thing like Olivia. Yet she zipped along on narrow, hedge-lined roads without issue.

After nearly an hour of silence, she surprised me. Or perhaps it was an attempt to distract me.

"Do you ever think about our time together?"

"The first few years, yeah, a lot. Then I moved to a different life altogether and I no longer thought about it. Neither the good nor the bad parts. What about you?"

"No, not really. Sometimes just brief glimpses of something fun we did. Then recently I thought a lot about it and realized I've forgotten blocks of that time."

"It happens. It was a long time ago so no wonder your memory is spotty."

"One thing I remember is that you were smitten with me."

"My mistake was falling in love."

"Not very smart of you was it."

"Weren't you in love?"

"Of course. I fell first, almost as soon as I met you. Unlike you."

"You grew on me. We were fun together, but I didn't know you were in love with me. But then I fell for you. I guess it was about the same time you were having buyer's remorse."

"Yes, my better sense kicked in."

"Oh, so that is what it was. Your better sense. I always thought it was that British guy with money."

"No, I won't take part in that argument again. Give it up."

"I will drop it because it doesn't matter. It didn't work out for you, and then you moved on."

"You still can't admit the whole thing was just a bad idea, can you? Yet another few months together and you would have come to the same conclusion."

"Possibly, but somewhere in my brain I always thought it could have worked."

"You thought it could have, but I realized it would not work."

"Obviously. And you will never tell me why."

"Perhaps I can't remember, but it doesn't matter. Still, you were once smitten," she said teasingly.

"You have the verb tense correct. But at this age, smart far outweighs smitten."

"It does, doesn't it? But it is a shame in a way. Takes the fun out of things."

"And takes the risk out as well. I would like fun without risk. Maybe I have become like you."

"Whilst perhaps I've become how you used to be."

"Ironic, huh? But I don't think so. You will always be the practical sort."

"You mean taking care of myself?"

"I think so. But I don't know you anymore." I wanted to move our conversation on and away from her slightly flirty teasing. Knowing it meant nothing, but still it made me slightly uncomfortable.

"We were dumb twenty-somethings. Drinking too much and exploring things as we should have while young. Then you suggested marriage."

"It was a bit of a joke as I remember."

"Not enough of one, apparently. It seemed like only a minute later we were at the civil office and making your joke official."

"It took two to sign the papers."

"Exactly what I was going to say. Just like it took two to sign the divorce decree."

"I was sorry about that."

I laughed, not in a mean way. "Olivia, a woman is rarely sorry when getting a divorce. I rather remember you being quite relieved."

"Yes, I admit I was relieved. What I was sorry about was how it all happened, how it must have made you feel."

"You know what? The divorce wasn't the worst part."

"Oh? What was?"

"Remember the day we were in France, just after it was official. Our last quick trip together, platonic, to tie up loose ends. You told me you would never contact me again."

"I do recall that."

"Probably because I was so stunned, I made you say it again."

"I probably shouldn't have said it, but it made sense as a way to close things off."

"Yes, but the actuality of it was something different to me."

"Please explain."

"What you said meant you no longer considered us married, of course. But also we were not friends, not colleagues, not even acquaintances. I was nothing to you. Nothing. From everything to nothing in months."

"That is not how I meant it."

"It was how I took it. And I think a part of you meant it that way."

She said nothing else. I suppose she was processing it, or maybe didn't want to admit it was true.

"James. You must think me a terrible person. And, I did... I did contact you."

"Only to keep you out of jail, decades later."

"Ah, now I see your demand for professionalism."

"Safer for both of us. And I admit, safer more for me than you."

"You don't know that."

"I recall that you were ever the practical one. I doubt that has changed. And we keep getting off on this useless tangent instead of exonerating you. We need to be focused on that. Stiff upper lip and all."

"Yes, just like your stiff upper lip."

"I don't have that affliction."

"James, since you have been here you have not touched me. Not a handshake, a hug, or a kiss on the cheek. Why not?"

"I don't think it prudent. Strictly professional will get us through this."

"See, the stiff upper lip, Americano style."

"We've touched in the past. It didn't work out."

"What, you think if you touch me I'll throw myself upon you?"

"I don't think you would. But like I said, I'm keeping it professional."

The conversation stopped, and I was content with the renewed silence. Slowly, the high ridges yielded to rolling hills and more houses and neighborhoods. Olivia took a route to go around Manchester to miss the worst of the traffic. We stopped for coffee for me, and tea for her along the way in Warrington. We would have dinner later in Macclesfield. I noticed that even at the shop she was quieter than normal. Perhaps she was dreading going to the Macclesfield house. From what little I knew, it was his residence, while Olivia stayed in Keswick. The reason for the split was still to be determined, but it should explain why Olivia was not a grieving widow.

We passed through Macclesfield town proper, and into the community just past it. On the edge, Olivia pulled into a gated drive. A brick wall shielded the house and grounds from the road. She pressed digits on the keypad and the wooden gate bound with iron opened. Olivia drove past a small carriage house on the right, and a manicured lawn and gardens appeared to the left, in front of the residence. We stopped in front of a stately brick home. The setting was very nice and the house was big enough, but a step down from a palatial estate like the footballers maintained.

CHAPTER TEN

We stopped in front of the house on the circular drive. "Welcome to the manor," Olivia said. "You can ramble around for a while then I'll fetch you for dinner."

"Aren't you going to show me around?"

"Of course I am. Otherwise you'll waste time and probably get lost between the kitchen and dining room. First I'll show you where to put your bag."

"I thought it would go with yours." I saw a slight tic across Olivia's face as she paused speechless. Then I laughed. She started to, but then turned around without a word. She unlocked the door and I followed her through the foyer and upstairs.

"This is your room for the evening," she said and opened the door to a nice bedroom. "I'm at the end of the hall."

"I suppose this is where our bags part ways. A shame since they seemed so compatible together riding down here in the boot."

"Things are not always as they seem. I'll find you later. Campbell's study is downstairs, at the back of the foyer take the door to the left."

"Are we dressing for dinner?"

"Casual tonight. It's a place you will like." She walked to her room with no further comment. I was not sure whether my earlier tease had angered her or caused some other reaction. Then again, she had also been quiet at times in the car. I put the bag on the bed and took out clothes to hang and slightly unwrinkle.

My first stop was not the study, but outside. I walked the grounds encircling the house. An old brick outbuilding was behind the house but held nothing of interest. I went to the carriage house and again found nothing useful. The yard and gardens were nice but I doubt Campbell had ever cut a blade of grass or pruned a shrub. Gardeners had done all this and there was nothing of the owner here.

Back inside the house I went from room to room downstairs. Each room was meticulously decorated and held not a gram of personality. It might as well have been a museum. The study was my last stop. Finally, some personal touches became evident. The artwork on the walls was different, with personal photographs instead of paintings of the countryside, manor houses, dogs, and horses. The photos were of groups of people, most with Campbell included. In front of stately buildings, a boat, what looked to be a pheasant hunt, and in two board-rooms. What I did not see were any family photographs.

I systematically started going through every drawer in the room. The desk, the display cabinet, and the filing drawers. I checked under and in the cushion of the desk chair and the leather sofa in the room. Each wall hanging was taken down so I could check the back. I looked under the rugs and would have checked the wastebasket but it was empty. My reward for the search was nothing.

I went back to the desk and went through it again. Each drawer was removed and I used my phone flashlight to peer into the bowels of the desk. I took everything off the desk and pushed it over on its front so I could see if there was anything underneath it, either on the floor or taped to the bottom of the wood. Finding nothing, I turned the desk upright and replaced the drawers.

I began to take all the ballpoint pens apart. Then the tape dispenser and stapler. I found a small strip of paper inside the stapler, stuck under the row of staples once I removed them. That is when I realized it was the first piece of paper I had come across in the entire office. There was not a single book, calendar, notebook, pad, newspaper, scrap or anything made from cellulose in the room. It had already been scoured clean.

I unfolded the tiny piece of paper. I assumed it was a product code for which replacement staples to use. Instead, written in small precise letters were three words with a number beside each. The list was BMK 17; MAPA 28;

Tartaric 43. The last one seemed familiar, if it referred to tartaric acid, but I didn't know what the list meant, if anything. But it had been hidden in the stapler for a reason. I put it back as I had found it after taking a picture with my phone. I would research it later. I was out of ideas of where to search inside the room. I saw the vent as the residence used a central heat system. I took off the cover and reached in as far as possible after shining my phone light inside. I found nothing and replaced the cover.

I heard movement upstairs and Olivia called out for me. I answered, and she told me it was time for dinner. She came down dressed casually so I didn't feel the need to change clothes. She grabbed a light jacket and we went to the car.

"Did you find anything?" she asked. "From the sounds, you must have spent time taking apart the study."

"Not much. Obviously someone went through and stripped every scrap of paper in the room."

"Really? The police searched it and took all the computer equipment and paper files, but left the blank books, notes and bills."

"Well, someone else came back and emptied the place. None of that is there now. Any idea who might have access?"

"Myself, the kids, and the couple that looks after the house and grounds."

"Then no one that would strip the study of all paper."

"No. Why would someone do that?"

"They were looking for something for themselves or preventing someone else from finding something."

"I doubt Campbell had anything fitting either scenario."

"But somebody thought he did. Did the police come back after the first search?"

"Not to my knowledge."

"I don't think we are going to find out. But you might want to update the security system and change the locks."

"We don't have a security system. After this trip I probably won't be back. I'd rather sell the property."

"Even better. Now, let's go eat."

Olivia drove us toward Macclesfield but turned off the road in the first community before entering town. More turns and she pulled up to an old building. I studied it then began to laugh.

"What is so funny?" Olivia asked.

"I've been here before."

"What? When?"

"Some years ago, when I came to a meeting up at Shrigley Hall. Had a nice dinner here and my first local-made cloudy cider. Ended up being my drink of choice."

"You were here but didn't let me know."

"Of course not, why would I? We'd been divorced for years and remember, you said you never wanted to talk to me again."

Olivia said nothing further as we got out of the car. I could have said the place looked just the same, but honestly I could not remember much about it. Just the meal that night was good and the cider phenomenal. Once seated, Olivia continued her silence while perusing the menu. I did not feel the need to break the silence. I ordered a cider of course and Olivia ordered a scotch, and we both ordered a meal.

"James, I don't want to go back over the past again."

"Neither do I. But it finds us anyway. You have to admit this is quite a coincidence."

"I suppose. Yet while it should be funny, I feel more of a lingering sadness."

"It is what happens when two people meet an abrupt end, then they keep on living separate lives without resolution of that conflict. At least that is my take."

"True enough. But I don't like being sad, regardless of the reason. Although I know I was the cause in our case. I did what I felt to be right."

"If you think you caused your own sadness, I'm not sure how I can help."

"You can't, I just need to get over it."

"Could you ever have imagined us sitting together in this place for dinner? Whether last week or last decade?"

"No, I could not. But there have been times…"

"There were times when you what?" It wasn't like Olivia to ever second-guess herself.

"Never mind. It means nothing and thinking on it doesn't help."

The food arrived, and we went quiet again. The conversation was going nowhere. Olivia might have once had feelings for me and could have even had second thoughts. But she was who she was and nothing would ever change that. And I had to admit, after the bittersweet few days of getting to know her again, I don't think it would have ever worked out, then or now. I reckoned she knew that full well and had acted on it long ago.

The food was good, and the cider was still excellent. Rare for me I ordered a second. Olivia was on her third scotch. But I knew she could hold her liquor. If not, we'd be taking a taxi back as I'd not be driving.

As with many establishments I had dined in around the UK, the bar was in an adjoining room and mostly open to the dining room. I saw a young man come in that looked familiar, but I could not place him. I put it out of my mind and decided to try my luck with riling my dining partner. Sometimes it was a useful strategy to pry information from an unwilling source.

"This must be difficult for you," I said. It was time to wander into the minefield. I blamed it on the second cider affecting my mental acuity.

"How so?"

"Bringing an ex-husband, a person you don't know anymore, into your dead husband's house. A man you obviously cared for so little that perhaps you did do him harm. And although I'm here under the guise of looking for clues to his death, perhaps my role is to help you cover it up."

Olivia was speechless. She finally downed the scotch and ordered another. I think I was about to get left at the restaurant.

"You always had the ability to cut right to the heart of an issue," she finally said. "Despite any damage that might come to the people around you."

"It is a blessing and a curse. I'm old enough to know the harm it can cause. But I really want to know your honest response to what I said. For once."

"Fine. All of this has been hard for me. I don't like what you said. I'm angry at you, at me, and at the situation I find myself in. Whatever happened to Campbell on that ridge, it was not my doing, nor do I know about it. And I hope you can prove it before you drive me mad."

"Thank you."

"For what?"

"For telling me the truth."

"I'm not a heartless automaton. But I refuse to show my emotions regardless of my anger. Anything else you like to say or ask?"

"No. You've told me what I need to know."

She downed her current scotch, paid for dinner and we left. There was no further conversation. At the house she went straight to her room while I went to the kitchen to find water, tea, or whatever to drink. I felt bad about the earlier conversation but I had to pierce the emotionless veil she had raised ever since I had arrived. I was worried that was who she was now. I didn't think she was a murderer, but she could have been playing me. Tonight, I heard the hurt in her voice and for the first time believed what she told me, at least in regard to Campbell. It was not a nice thing to do, and I'm sure someone else could have been more empathetic or smooth. But I did not have those skills so I used what I could.

I took my bottled water upstairs. I heard something from Olivia's room and went closer. At the door I heard her crying. I knocked softly and went in. She was on the bed in a robe and gown. She gave me a look that clearly told me to go away. As usual I ignored it and sat beside her.

"James, go away, leave me alone."

"Not a chance." I put my arm around her. She did not resist or say anything. Just more crying.

"I have not cried since the children were little," she said. "I don't know what is wrong with me."

For the first time, I said nothing at all. Anything from my mouth would have been wrong. Instead I continued holding her. She smelled wonderful and felt warm and soft on my arm. Despite the crying she was still beautiful. It was like a setup from an old movie. The big difference was that I didn't want her. I could comfort her but that was all.

The next morning I woke up with Olivia's head on my arm. We were still clothed and lying on top of the covers. We had passed the night together, platonically, after she cried herself out. I looked down to see her awake and studying me.

"Thank you," she said.

"For what exactly?"

"For being there for me. For not taking advantage of the situation."

"You are welcome. Also, at the risk of saying this badly, I'm not interested."

"Ouch. You must have been waiting years to say that."

"No, just since last night. I finally realized what you knew more than thirty years ago. You were right, it would never have worked. Still won't."

"James?"

"Yes."

"That's the worst morning after bedroom talk ever."

I laughed. "It is, even for me. Does your glimpse of humor mean that you are back?"

"I think so. A good cry was more therapeutic than I imagined."

"I think I shall try it."

"Please wait until you get home."

"I will. Oh, there is still something I need to do. Was this Campbell's bedroom?"

"It is or was."

"I need to go through it before we leave."

"Can it wait until I'm showered and dressed?"

"It could, but I'd not see anything I haven't already seen."

"Get out you cad."

"Yes dear."

After Olivia went downstairs I tossed the room. I found exactly nothing. Once again, no paper of any sort, not even tissue. I checked the bathroom and toilet paper was present. It was the only paper in either room. Somebody was thorough in removing it all.

Downstairs Olivia was making breakfast. English bacon and scrambled eggs, toast and tea. "Somebody worked up an appetite last night," I said.

"Don't start with me."

"I would not dream of it."

"You know, if you had shown the least interest last night, you truly would have needed this breakfast." She held my look of disbelief before cracking a smile.

"At least you can still tease me," I said.

"We were good at it once."

"Life got in the way. You can't tease someone when you or they are hurting."

"No, you cannot. Unless you are a monster."

"I don't think either of us shrank to that point."

"We didn't. Now we should eat and I'll drive us back to Keswick. Unless you'd like to try your luck driving the road."

"Not if we both want to keep breakfast down."

CHAPTER ELEVEN

The trip back to Keswick was uneventful. We occasionally talked, but we were comfortable enough with each other again that we didn't need to. As we neared the Lake District, I thought it time to pursue another line of inquiry. I wanted to visit the nearest train station, which was in Penrith. There was a slim chance there could be video footage of one or more people involved with Campbell's death. I had already checked the train schedules from a few different locations arriving into Penrith the night of his death. I knew the time frame I wanted to view with Olivia's help, and the times I wanted to watch the footage by myself. Although I thought she would be resistant to my visit, she was surprisingly helpful.

"Olivia, do you know anyone at the Penrith Station?"

"I believe so. Why?"

"I would like to go there and worm my way into the manager's good graces."

"James, I'd be happy to take you there. But I doubt you often obtain anyone's good graces."

"Do you think anyone at the station would let me look at camera footage?"

"I can almost guarantee it. I assure you it won't be a problem." She seemed confident so she must know something I did not. Another secret that I would have to observe or ferret out myself. Olivia kept up her annoying traits. "Shall I drop you at the Clareridge or do you want to come to the house?"

"The Inn is fine. I have a couple of things to attend to. Do you think we might visit the station tomorrow?"

"Possibly. I'll text you if I hear back by then."

At the Inn I sent a message back to Warm Springs. I needed all the help I could get, however unlikely the outcome might be. Maybe Millard's braintrust of octogenarian experts could make some sense of Campbell Stewart and the message from the stapler. I still had not come up with a name for Millard's group, but was leaning toward OctoPosse. I didn't know if they would be delighted or offended by that moniker. But I'd use it anyway.

It was an easy ride to Penrith the next day. Olivia drove while I stared out the window, paying just enough attention to what Olivia was saying to keep up the pretense of a conversation. I really would rather have viewed the scenery, but I had to keep up appearances.

"Olivia, if I get to see the video footage, would it be possible for you to distract anyone else that might be around during the viewing? I'd like to do it in private if possible."

"You mean in case you see something that others should not?"

"Exactly. Since I don't know what, if anything, is on there, better to keep it among us."

"I will make it happen. It should not be too hard. When you are ready for me to do it, say something like chopsticks or mustard."

"That's kind of silly, but it should work. How about flapjack?"

"OK, I'll remember that."

After parking, we entered the station together. It was not a large station but much bigger than either Windermere station or the Keswick bus stop. An older brick building fronted the street with an underground walkway to get over to the other platform for additional trains. The waiting areas along the bays were covered by an old metal superstructure with glass windows.

We entered through the main front door, and I noticed a camera above. I saw another out in the car park covering the only other exit from the station. Another was inside, and a fourth directed onto the train bays. That one should give a clear view of anyone getting off a train. The one in the car park would give a view of a person meeting others or getting picked up.

Olivia led us to an unmarked door beside the ticket

counter. Inside was a desk with a receptionist. The woman recognized Olivia and they exchanged pleasantries.

"Is Mr. Byrd in his office?" Olivia asked. "We had planned to meet this morning."

"Yes, he is. Let me announce you then please go in."

A moment later we were in a small office with dark wood panels, making the space feel even more claustrophobic. A smaller man rose and gave Olivia a hug, lasting more than three seconds. He finally released and gave me a glance and brief handshake.

"Mr. Byrd, this is James Wilder. Dr. Wilder is a family friend from America. He is also an investigator working for me. You must have heard about the death of Campbell, my husband. Dr. Wilder is looking into his whereabouts the day before he fell. Can you speak with him, please? Please feel free to tell him anything you would tell me. If within your power, please grant him any requests as you would me."

"Mrs. Stewart, I was sorry to hear about Mr. Stewart. I would be glad to speak with Dr. Wilder. I'm not sure what I can do, but I shall do everything I can to assist. Dr. Wilder, how can I help?" I noticed he used Mrs. Stewart instead of Dr. Stewart to address Olivia.

"I would like to see the video from the station's exit camera, or any footage of the station or surroundings you may have. Specifically, for the evening of Campbell's death."

Byrd did not say anything, but I thought he appeared worried. I doubt citizens, or Americans, normally asked for the video surveillance footage. Therefore I needed to give him a viable explanation, even if I was lying.

"I am not looking for any evidence of a crime. Campbell's car was not found near where he fell. Therefore I am looking for any evidence he might have met someone such as his assistant that might have dropped him off that evening before leaving the car at the trail exit." It was a weak lie, but I hoped just enough to get Byrd to allow me to view the video.

"I see," he said. I doubted that he did, since I did not. "What if you did see any evidence of a crime?"

"That is not my area of involvement. Either you or Mrs. Stewart would have to take that to the authorities, and I would excuse myself from the situation."

"Very well, I believe I can accommodate your request. Follow me to the viewing room."

The viewing room title was misleading. More of a hall closet with no ventilation, an ancient video machine, and a desktop computer with monitor.

"I'll show you our computer filing system. We keep a copy of the video for one month, then reuse the memory disks to be efficient. The evening you are seeking should be here, under this label date. There are four cameras, labeled in order of train yard number one, out to the car park as number four. Once you access the date and camera, you'll have to fast forward to your time frame. Any questions, or do you need my receptionist to assist?"

"I think I can handle the filing system. I will ask however if I run into something difficult. I do have a question about an entirely unrelated topic. As an American, I cannot get flapjacks at home. Are there any bakeries in town that sell them?

"I believe so. There is one, two blocks down Ullswater Road."

"Mr. Byrd, I would also like to visit the bakery," Olivia said. "Would you accompany me so we can catch up?"

"Olivia, that is a splendid idea. I'd love to, and we can come back through Castle Park. Dr. Wilder, please ask my receptionist if you need help."

"Gladly, Mr. Byrd."

As they left, I noticed Byrd was glowing like a schoolboy who had just scored a prom date. I got down to the business of finding the correct files, which was easy. The tedious part was watching the videos of people I didn't know. And knowing the whole thing could be a waste of time since no suspect, or one that I knew, might have come through the station.

After people left the train, they made their way through one opening from the train bay area into the old station building. The inside camera had a perfect view of the people moving through the doorway mostly single file. The two cameras outside the building gave me two views of the sidewalk, the other exit, and the car park. I could see a view of whether they went to the bus stop, got in a taxi, walked away, or were picked up. I could also see the faces of people coming into the station doorway. All good information, I just had to wade through it all.

I began, fast forwarding to the time when I thought the video might yield results. There were not many passengers getting off the train at this stop at the times I reviewed. Spotting a particular person was easy as they filed out the train and into the building under the camera's view.

Moments after one train arrived I saw what I came to

see. Not what I wanted to see, but it was what I expected. It was also not what I had told either Olivia or Mr. Byrd that I was looking for. I was about to turn off the video but decided to watch for other trains due that evening around the same time. The second sighting surprised me. I replayed the video to make sure of what I saw. The plot had just thickened, and a new player was afoot. I realized what I had just thought and figured the English whodunit caper was brainwashing me.

Then another surprise as I looked at the car park camera. A young man was there, hanging about and watching cars. The same one I noticed in the Keswick shops, and in the bar in Macclesfield where Olivia and I dined. He was obviously involved in this business, but whether he was a criminal or a policeman, I had no idea.

I now had three suspects and no idea of what to do about them. I turned off everything and went to Byrd's office. I heard Olivia laughing as I got there.

"Oh, James, have you finished already?" she asked.

"I believe so. The evening tapes show no one of interest."

"Well, Mr. Byrd, my thanks for humoring us," Olivia said.

"Yes, thank you, Mr. Byrd," I said.

"Glad to be of service, Dr. Wilder. Olivia I'm sorry for your loss, but it has been a delight seeing you. Please let me know if you need anything."

"I will, and thank you again, Mr. Byrd." She hugged him and he held it again for longer than convention required.

Back in the car, I decided to poke the bear. "How do you know him, Olivia?"

"Campbell was on the Board that oversaw Penrith. Mr. Byrd is on the Board as befits his position as station manager. I attended quarterly meetings with Campbell and a social event was held after each meeting. The past couple of years I attended sporadically as Campbell no longer attended. He would have soon lost that position but he never cared about it anyway."

"Ah, so you got to hang out with Byrd. He is an odd little fellow and a bit clingy. Is he a little sweet on the widow Stewart?"

"Please, don't make me nauseous. But I will play that card if I have to."

"Why Olivia, using your feminine wiles on the lonely station keeper. I am aghast."

"Get over it, James. You would do the same if you had to. And if you keep teasing me, you won't get the flapjack I bought for you."

"Yes I have done the same, and will again. Needs must." She stared at me but did not bother replying. "How does one get on a Board?" I asked.

"Know the right people from school, inherit a business, attend social events to network. Soon enough people think you are somebody important."

"At least he wasn't royalty."

"He was third or fourth in line as a baron or lord."

"I guess Ian then gets the honor."

"I doubt it. I believe he is sixteenth in line. It would require a significant plague to place him in that position."

"You can always hope."

"No, I won't. Those titles tend to draw sycophants and undesirable leches. I would never want that for Ian."

"But the Lady Olivia could use her title to quash dissent, and found a new empire of royalty to rule the kingdom."

"That is why I asked you here. You have astounding powers of deduction."

"Your sarcasm is why I will leave."

"You used to like it."

"I used to like beer. Then I realized what a shallow, gaseous, disgusting drink it was."

"Are you saying I'm gaseous and disgusting?"

"You forgot shallow."

"Yes, because I'm shallow as well."

"I'm not saying it. More of an implication." I got a slight smile from her. "Olivia, I would like to talk to Ian."

"I really don't think it necessary."

"Still, I'd like his perspective on Campbell's life and death."

"He's away at university and I'd prefer he not be disturbed. He has enough to deal with. Speaking with him would distract him from his studies."

"You really do not want me to meet or talk to him."

"I do not. It serves no purpose for your investigation but would bother him. I do not approve of your request."

"If you mean approve in the sense you don't like it, I understand. I f you mean it in the sense that you forbid me to do so, you know that will just propel me to do it anyway."

"You are right. Let me think about it and maybe he can meet when he has a light class day."

"Thanks." I knew a stall tactic when I heard it. Olivia wasn't ever going to find a good time for me to talk to Ian.

I suspected as much but wanted to give her the opportunity to agree, even if on her terms. She was not going to, so I would go around her.

Did you see anything of value on the tapes?" she asked.

"No. But it was a long shot anyway. Another box checked off at least." With all the lying and omissions flying around, I thought my lie would go unnoticed.

Back at the Inn I got a call from back home.

"James, I have some information for you regarding your note."

"Sure Millard, go ahead."

"We have a consensus that the most likely interpretation of your note is as follows. BMK is benzyl methyl ketone or phenylacetone. MAPA is methyl alpha-phenylacetoacetate. Tartaric is tartaric acid."

"Three chemicals. What does that mean?"

"Either of the two by themselves would likely mean nothing. The third, tartaric acid. I'm sure you know that one from your food background."

"Yes, I do know it."

"We believe the chemicals are key to the one of the few major methods of producing methamphetamines in Europe."

"Now that is interesting."

"The note was referring to two precursor chemicals and a cleaning agent chemical required for the process. Your guy was referring to or maybe making or supplying chemicals. We found he was the CEO of a chemical company, so he had access to them."

"OK, what I'm hearing is that these are three things commonly used to make meth in Europe."

"Yes. Two precursors to make the drug, and the third to clean it up. All three have been confiscated by police in large busts where they have tried to prevent manufacture of methamphetamines. If the person you are investigating is involved in the business he could have made a lot of money, but also risked discovery by the authorities."

"Is that something that could have gotten him killed?"

"Hard to know. Possibly if there was competition among groups trying to buy those chemicals. Certainly there would be enough money involved to cause problems."

"What about the numbers on the note?"

"They could refer to volume, price, quantity, or something else. We don't know without context."

"Did you find out anything about Campbell himself?"

"No, nothing beyond the usual information available on everyone online these days. As you already know, based on his type of business we believe he could be involved with manufacturing and supplying those items to the meth business. We have a list of things to check on your end which we are sending by email. Invoices, customs records, those types of things. Although you probably won't find anything because they would be hidden or falsified."

"I've checked his home office. Not a single piece of paper other than what I sent you."

"He could have been incredibly careful. Or more likely someone has already searched and confiscated all records."

"Exactly what I think. I will plan on going to his business soon. I've also noticed someone following me, but casually."

"Interesting. Bad guy or good guy?"

"No idea. And I would not know the difference anyway. But nothing threatening."

"If you see them again maybe you should approach and have a chat."

"That is a good idea. He probably won't talk to me but his demeanor should tell me which side he's on."

"That business in Warm Springs recently, with the murder and the pot busts. Those guys were amateurs compared to what we have heard about regarding the European methamphetamine crowd. Be careful over there."

"Thanks, Millard. That could help clear up some things. Be sure and give the guys, or girls, or both my thanks."

"I will. Good luck over there. Are you coming back soon? That cat of yours has about three people wanting her."

"Can't have that. I should be finishing up here soon. Three or four days at the most, then I should be home."

"See you when you get here."

I noticed Millard did not mention the package I left for him before my trip. That could be bad or good. Or maybe it was not important enough to even mention.

CHAPTER TWELVE

"James, I think you should take a walk with Elizabeth," Olivia said, while we sat in her front garden.

"Is that to punish me or her?"

"Both, of course. But I think she wants to ask you some things. Topics she is not comfortable asking when I'm around."

"You must be mistaken. She hates me and does not even know me."

"It is mostly an act on her part. If she thinks I like you then it is her duty to dislike you."

"You don't like me either."

"True, but you did come over to rescue me. She thinks there is still something between us."

"Poor deluded girl."

"Maybe, but she needs to get to know you enough to talk to you."

"I thought you wanted to keep everyone in your life far away from me to keep your secrets."

"I do, but Elizabeth is developing an interest in me, and by association, an interest in you."

"What makes you think that?"

"She starts to ask or say something, then stops. When she finally gets out a question about you I tell her I don't know, and then she storms off. Perhaps you could fill in the blanks."

"What have you told her about your youth, and about us?"

"Very little. I start to, but she acts embarrassed."

"And stomps off?"

"Her national pastime."

"But back to Elizabeth. Is there anything I should not tell her?"

"I don't think so. The time for secrets regarding us is over. Be as frank as you want. Or as she demands."

"She does not look much like you. I assume she looks like her father."

"I hear that a lot. No, not much like her father. But does resemble her grandmother."

"Ah, a throwback. Genes recombined to honor the prior generation."

"I suppose. It's always been a joke within the family."

Later, Elizabeth drove us to the dock on Derwentwater.

She had already purchased tickets online and had them on her phone. I stood and admired the island across the water. Elizabeth was more focused on the lonely rows of broken pilings leading from near us out into the lake a hundred feet or more before disappearing. The skeleton of a much grander, or at least longer dock, I guessed.

Once the long wooden powerboat arrived, we boarded and took it across the lake. We planned to ascend the ridge and walk around half the lake and back to the car. If we tired or the weather turned bad, we could also drop back down to the lake at two different points to catch the boat back to the Derwentwater dock. Between the short drive over and waiting for the boat, Elizabeth had said little. It was a bit noisy on the boat so I didn't attempt a conversation. I assumed she would speak or ask questions on her own timetable.

We stepped off the boat on a short dock across the lake. A trail meandered up the ridge before us. Just from habit I checked my small pack once more. I doubted the beautiful early fall weather would turn nasty, but these ridges had lied to me before. Elizabeth noticed my actions.

"You don't have to worry," Elizabeth said. "The weather will stay pleasant."

"I expect it will. But I'll be ready nonetheless." We began up the hill.

"I don't think today will bring storms."

"Did your mom ever tell you about the time we hiked on a beautiful day, then got stuck on a ridgetop, threatened by lightning and pummeled by sleet?"

"No she did not."

"It can happen out here. Not often, but the storms from

the coast can get here and turn your day around in twenty minutes. Well before you can get off the ridge if it comes from behind the next ridge over. Coming that direction you get about five minutes warning."

"It hasn't happened to me yet, but I've heard stories."

"The stories are true."

"Why didn't you stay with my mother?"

"That came from left field. Very direct as well. What has she told you?"

"She told me a little. But not much so I know she is hiding a lot."

"I would have stayed. I thought she was the one for me. But she went dead on us. Whatever passion, love, lust, or infatuation she had for me, it just disappeared. I don't remember daily details, but it happened quick enough."

"That must have been devastating."

"It was."

"Is that why you are here, to solve that mystery?"

"That is very insightful. But no, not really. I don't believe that mystery will ever be solved. The only person that knows the answer isn't talking."

"She's like that. Full of secret things that close her off to the people around her."

"She has her reasons, I do know that."

"Oh, so you have secrets too, but about her. Why not tell me?"

"Those are only for her to reveal. Or not as she sees fit."

"You are just as frustrating as she is."

"I have no business telling anyone, including her daughter, some of those things she wishes to keep silent. Think about it, I knew her for two years, many years ago. I'm not the one to divulge anything. I don't even know if there are any secrets anymore. Or what those secrets could lead to. They could be worth nothing, or they might be even more devastating than she once thought. No, me saying anything is not worth the risk."

"Oh, she still has them, bound tight and quiet. But I understand your reluctance."

"Thank you."

"Maybe she cut you off because you knew her secrets."

"That has occurred to me more than once. But again, only she knows why."

"Maddening she is at times. We got along when I was young. I was lucky to have a good mother, especially compared to my friends. We did not get along much in my teens. But lately we have gotten closer. My being away seemed to help. Then with all that is happening now, we are back to worse than ever."

"That's common enough among mothers and daughters, as well as fathers and sons."

"Do you have children?"

"Sorry, I'm not answering any questions about family."

"What?"

"I've already explained to Olivia. We won't get involved in each other's lives, including talking about family. If you had not been at home during this time you'd likely have never known I had been here."

"You are both insane. Two people walking around and not talking, full of secret vaults."

"That has been said before."

"What did my grandparents think of you?"

"I never met Olivia's father. Her mother was polite enough."

"I have never met him either. Mum made sure of that. More family secrets. But I can see Nana being polite. Just enough not to skewer you."

"My opinion was she didn't like Americans. Something about her mother being involved with one, maybe during the war."

"Oh good, another secret. I'll try and pry that one out of mum. Surely the statute of limitations has passed."

"True. Maybe you will get that one out of Olivia."

"You didn't know her very well did you?"

"Your mom?"

"Yes."

"In some ways I knew her better than anyone. But in other ways I did not know her at all."

"I feel exactly the same."

"She compartmentalizes. If you are approved for that compartment you get it all. If not, it is closed forever."

"That is very well put. It describes her exactly."

"As her daughter, you can accept that or fight it to no avail. But have some compassion. Even if she never tells you, she compartmentalizes to protect herself. And maybe to protect you and your brother."

"You know more than I do. You've been in those compartments I don't even know about."

"Perhaps. But don't envy me. Some things you can't unknow. Now, enough about Olivia and her secrets. Let us enjoy the day."

"You're still protecting her. After what she did to you and after all this time. You still love her."

"That is true. But without any illusions for what it means. I'll give a bad analogy. Did you have pets growing up?"

"Yes, a cat when I was little and dogs later."

"Did any of them disappear or die?"

"Yes."

"Yet you still feel a certain way for them, even though they are gone and never coming back. My old feelings are irrelevant. The pain recedes over time and it is easier to remember her more fondly."

"I guess I see your point."

"She's out of my life and never coming back, but I have some good memories of a brief time in my youth. Bad ones too, of course."

"But she's not out of your life. You are here and helping her."

"Ah, now you see why I'm keeping this on a professional basis. I can't afford to let her back in."

"So now you are here, but shutting her out of your life. Payback?"

"I'm trying for it not to be. Rather, I'm compartmentalizing."

"I see what you've done. We just went in a great big circle."

"Something like that. But do you understand a little more about her?"

"A little. And you too. You two must have been something in the day. You still make a handsome couple."

"Maybe."

"You do. You have not seen each other forever yet within minutes you're acting like best friends."

"I'm not sure I feel that myself. But I'll give you a free sample of what we were once like. Your one and only old story of reminiscence. We had taken a cheap flight over to Scandinavia. It was summer, and the warm days lasted forever. Before going back to the airport, we wandered around and found a Greek restaurant. We sat outside across from each other at a small table near the edge of the patio. After struggling to order Greek food in a foreign language, we sat talking quietly and drinking wine. Then we ate. We were dressed in regular clothes and acting completely normal. But from my vantage I noticed other people kept looking at us. Olivia brought it up first, telling me that the patrons were watching us. I told her the people behind her were acting the same way."

"Is that the end of the story?"

"Yes. Whatever we had during that time was magical. Anywhere we went we drew attention. I can't explain it, only describe it. Somehow our feelings for each other were bigger than us, maybe like we were giving off a glow or something, affecting those around us."

"That sounds lovely."

"It was, for a time. Whatever happens in your life, you should hope you find someone that you can achieve that with."

"Thank you, James. Your story gives me a glimpse into her life when she was younger and is something she never would have told me. I have never seen her like that. Reserved and borderline unhappy is her norm."

"At the time she wasn't too much older than you are now. She can be happy when she lets herself."

"What are you saying?"

"Appreciate your mother for who she is. But you don't have to be like her. You can choose to be happy and stay that way through life. Trust me, you will be better off if you can do that. She got off to a bad start that is always with her. From what little I know your start has been easier, although I could be wrong. But life is hard enough especially as you age. Choosing to be happy is your best defense."

"Words of wisdom from an American that could have been my dad."

"The only part of that statement that is true is that I am American. Words of wisdom usually are not going to come from me."

"Mum says you are safe."

"What does that mean?"

"I'm not sure, but she has used that phrase a few times over the years. Usually about men that I know. One of my uncles, and another was a family friend. Is she telling me that I'm safe with them because they won't try something?"

I did not say anything. It was dangerous ground, edging on an explosive compartment of Olivia's I wasn't sure anyone but me knew about.

"Your lack of an answer tells me a lot."

"I think your assessment is accurate. She is telling you something important."

"The part she said, or the part she implied?"

"Yes." We had arrived at the top of the ridge. Lines if ridges were before us, and the lake and town of Keswick in a stunning panorama behind us. "We should take a few minutes and enjoy this view."

Elizabeth did not say anything else, but I could tell she

was deep in thought. I had revealed nothing, but she had already come to the right conclusion. Something she had probably known all along. She was finally realizing she might share more with her mother, in regard to keeping secrets, than she previously thought. Somehow I knew their secrets however incredibly unlikely it should have been. Olivia had survived a tragic childhood, betrayed by the one person that should have protected her. And Elizabeth may well have killed the person that filled the same role in her life.

CHAPTER THIRTEEN

"Olivia, what kind of relationship did Elizabeth and Ian have with Campbell?"

"Relatively normal for the most part I would say. Typical friction as you would expect as the kids got older and Campbell disciplined them."

"How about your relationship with Campbell?"

"As I've mentioned, we were a typical couple. Lots of passion when we met, which diminished the past few years. Lately we had seen less of each other."

"And what about the interactions of the kids with their father with you around?"

"I'm not sure what you mean."

"Did the kids act differently when they were with their father than when all four of you were together?"

"I can't answer that question."

"Why not?"

"Because the kids have not seen their father in ages."

"What?"

"They don't have a relationship with him."

I had to take a minute and recompose myself. "Olivia, are you saying Campbell is not their father?"

"Exactly. He is, or was their stepfather."

"Did you not think that was important enough to tell me?"

"I didn't think it mattered."

"Maybe it does not. But maybe it does. I can't put a profile together of Campbell that means anything if I don't know key facts. I need an accurate profile so I can look for aberrations and anomalies that may point to factors of his death. I certainly need to differentiate between their father and stepfather. And just maybe their father could be a suspect."

"I'm sorry, I didn't know it was necessary."

"OK, so who is the father of your children?"

"His name is David Gatwick. He has not been in our lives since I started seeing Campbell."

"Tell me about him, about you and him, and how he got along with the kids. And tell me why he is no longer in your lives."

"See, those are specific things I can work with. You just have to tell me what you need."

"Do you notice my exasperation?"

"I do. I'll try to be more accommodating to your poor communication skills."

I thought she might be teasing me but I was past playing along with her. "Just tell me all about David."

"I met him in Belfast. He was at a meeting I attended. He was from Birmingham and we started dating. After a few months we got married."

"Was that the same meeting in Belfast where we mostly ended things? Before we went to France to officially kill it."

"I don't remember, a lot of those meetings run together."

"Yeah, OK. Proceed."

"After four years we decided to have kids. It was harder than we imagined. Lack of sleep, lack of money, too much togetherness. We ended up fighting more than anything else. Finally we decided on divorce. But we stayed friendly at first as he saw the kids regularly. He kept them when I traveled."

"And the kids liked him?"

"Yes, they did."

"I assume things were stable until you met Campbell."

"Yes. After I met Campbell as you might expect I was spending more and more time with him. David, I think was jealous. About the time Campbell and I got engaged, David ghosted us and disappeared. Other than sending the kids a birthday or Christmas card he was gone."

"How did the kids respond?"

"Not well. I don't believe they ever got over it."

"You said you thought he was jealous of Campbell. Did you ask him?"

"Not that I remember."

"Then you don't know why he left. Did you ever ask him later?"

"I haven't talked to him at all."

"Do you find any of that strange?"

"I don't know, perhaps. I had other things going on between raising the children and seeing Campbell."

"How can I find him?"

"Why do you need to? He's not going to be able to help with anything."

"I think it is very important that I talk to him."

"You might ask Elizabeth. She may have his cards with his address."

I thought of a lot of other questions I could ask, but I decided against it. I already was thinking of strangling Olivia. Was she that obtuse or was something else happening, regarding her lack of knowledge about her children's father?

"Thanks, I'll talk to Elizabeth."

"You seem cross."

"I'm stunned by your lack of curiosity or empathy in this particular case. I know that sounds harsh, but I mean it in a positive way." She left the room in a huff.

Something was going on with the family dynamic. Whether it had anything to do with Campbell's death was unknown, but I needed to either rule it out or in. Now I needed to find David. He could even be a suspect. At the least, I wanted to know why a man that had a good relationship with his children would ghost them. I could understand him ditching Olivia. But not the kids, unless he had a good reason. I went to find Elizabeth. Maybe she was the sane one in the house.

"You look angry," Elizabeth said after she answered my knock on her door.

"I had a conversation with your mother."

"That would do it. She's maddening."

"I have to agree. She finally told me Campbell was your stepfather. I should have known that days ago."

"You really didn't know?"

"No, who was going to tell me? I trusted your mother to tell me all the important details in your lives."

"And how did that go? You really cannot rely on her to give an accurate portrayal of our lives."

"I'm beginning to see that. Could you tell me about your father?"

"I could. Then I could take you to see him, if you wanted."

"That would be great. You can tell me about him on the way."

"Sure, I'll call and ask him if he's available today or tomorrow. Then we'll go see him."

Elizabeth and I took the bus and train to Bolton, north of Manchester. An easy two hours of travel. We ended up in front of a typical two-story row house with a car out front. A shopping district was a short walk away. The train station was within a long walk. Very middle class Britain.

Elizabeth had given me background on her father during the trip down. My impression was he was a very average guy and Elizabeth was relatively close to him the past few years. I wondered if that was since Olivia and Campbell had separated but I didn't ask. Elizabeth knocked on the door and it opened immediately.

David was slightly on the tall side and thinner, with

brown hair that might have some red tint, and brown eyes. Both kids definitely looked more like him than Olivia. He hugged Elizabeth and we shook hands. Inside, he offered Elizabeth some cash and told her to go shopping so we could talk. She took the hint and the cash and exited.

"Elizabeth tells me you came over to help Olivia out of her current jam," David said.

"I suppose that is accurate enough. Although I know she usually does not need much help."

"That is true. Very resourceful when she needs to be."

"And discreet, even when she should not be. Until yesterday I didn't know you existed. She let me believe Campbell was Ian and Elizabeth's father."

"I don't doubt it. Once she had someone she thought better, I was made redundant. Then disappeared from her orbit."

"I know exactly how that feels."

"Elizabeth said you were married to Olivia briefly. You might be the chap she left when we got together."

"Possibly. Just glad I didn't impregnate her. Less sticky that way."

"Oh, you are him, I think. And you are right about things getting sticky with Olivia. I love my kids, don't get me wrong. But my mistake was having them with her. She's not much for loyal. I found out later she was seeing Campbell before we ended things. Ironic, huh?"

"Yeah, we both know about how she operates. What is your story with Olivia since then?"

"Why are you asking?"

"I'm trying to figure out more about Campbell's death. Who might have done it if not an accident."

"You think I did it?"

"I absolutely have no idea. Did you? If you confess it would save me a lot of time."

"You have a strange sense of humor."

"I have to, since I must deal with Olivia. She led me on for days, having me believe the kids were Campbell's. Even after I found out she seemed to have no memory of you, or didn't think there was anything worth mentioning."

"Wow, you fight dirty. But I also know you are telling the truth about her. Just how she is. What do you want to know?"

"I understand how Olivia is, I really do. But from all accounts, you were a good dad. Then Campbell came around and you disappeared according to Olivia. Elizabeth would not say what happened. But I'm guessing there is a lot more to the story."

"He banished me from their lives, at least outwardly. He had the connections to make me a target. Get me fired or evicted. He could also use the kids against me. So on the surface, as far as Campbell and Olivia knew, I was gone."

"Could he have done that?"

"You're an American so you might not know all the British tricks. Yeah, he went to all the right schools, knew the right people, kept up with the right business crowd. He could have done that, back then before I was established. But he also threatened the kids. Told me how he would lock them in, take things away, make them miserable. I believed he would have."

"What about Olivia?"

"She was good with everything that happened, or maybe she didn't want to know. Selective knowledge."

"I did not think of her as obsessed with money."

"There is a bit of truth in that. She's not, at least not directly. But she cares about status, connections, things. And she claims it is for the kids. Again, a bit of truth as she is a good mum. But don't try and take any of those things away from her."

"She has a nice house and car. But doesn't seem like they were that wealthy."

"You are up in Keswick with her, right?"

"Yes."

"That is the summer house. You have not been to the other house."

"I didn't know there was another house." I did, but kept quiet to play along.

"Yes, the estate in Macclesfield. Campbell stayed down there most of the time, especially lately, while she stayed in Keswick."

"I had no idea. Her compartmentalization has gotten compulsive or she's intentionally hiding things from me."

"Is there a difference?"

"No, the outcome is the same. How did you deal with her? Or do you have any contact at all? She said she does not know anything about you."

"Mostly true. There was nothing there for me anymore and I risked seeing the kids hurt by Campbell. Better if I went away. Not that she really noticed or cared. I had to set up an elaborate system to keep up with the kids. Even then it was difficult to see them. As they got older it was easier. When Ian went to college we began seeing each other once or twice a month. Same with Olivia. Campbell quit caring or didn't feel the need to lord over them anymore."

"I think I dislike Campbell, even though he is dead."

"That would be a long queue to stand in. Other than his few equally unlikable friends, nobody cared for him."

"Hard to narrow down suspects in that case."

"Just about anyone who knew him is a suspect."

"What about Olivia?"

"No, not her. I think she actually liked him, in her own way. Or maybe the next thing hadn't come along yet. But now here you are at a good time in her life."

"Not a chance. Now or ever."

"She can be persuasive."

"Nope. I'd rather be drug through a cactus patch and dropped in a sewer."

"I'd say you learned your lesson the first time."

"I did. But one last question."

"Certainly."

"How did Ian and Elizabeth get along with Campbell, from your perspective."

I saw anger. "Best that you ask them. But do it carefully. I have nothing else to say about Campbell."

"I'll text Elizabeth and grab her on the way to the train station. Thanks for talking to me."

"Good luck, mate. You'll need it."

I had to play the part of a scorned ex during my conversation with David. In my view, it was easier to get him to talk to me. I didn't think Olivia was as bad as I had made her sound. Sure, she tended to value certain things in her life. She also devalued some people close to her. That made her very human. I went along with the conversation to keep him talking, and if he felt I was commiserating, then so be it. As it was, I did find out useful information.

I already knew about the Macclesfield house since Olivia had taken me there. David did confirm what I suspected, that Campbell had warned him off. Plus, Campbell's relationships with Ian and Elizabeth were strained. There must be a good reason for that but either David did not know or he did not want to tell me.

I had also wanted to meet and evaluate David as a suspect. I believed he had motive, at least in the past. But it did not make sense for David to kill him since Campbell was no longer keeping the older kids from their father. I was still surprised about Olivia's seeming lack of concern about David disappearing from his children's lives. Maybe she hated him or knew about Campbell's actions and did not want to cause problems for herself or the kids.

CHAPTER FOURTEEN

"James, I'd like to go sailing. Would you come with me?"

"Sure. But be warned, I know nothing about sailing."

"That's OK, it's a small boat and I can handle it myself. I can teach you the basics if you want to learn."

"I'd like that." Actually I wasn't sure that I wanted to sail, but I did want the chance to spend time with Elizabeth. I needed to understand who she was, and what she was capable of. "Is Olivia going?"

"Certainly not. She doesn't like it and would just weigh the boat down."

"Does the weather look good?"

"As good as it can in this season. We should be fine."

As little as I knew about sailing, I knew it was implied the boat would not have a motor. On a lake in the District, that could be a problem. I would pack appropriately.

"I need to get my bag from the Inn."

"Oh don't worry about it. We won't be gone long so you won't need anything. I'll bring lunch."

"Yet I still insist on my bag. Think of it as my purse, and we are going shopping."

"I concede. Get your bag if it makes you happy."

"I'll walk back to the Inn, so give me at least twenty minutes. Then we can take bikes to the marina."

At the Inn I packed up a small bag, just as if I was going on a ridge walk. It seemed prudent if we were out in the open lake with a motorless boat. Elizabeth seemed unconcerned with what could happen, and she might be right. But my nature prompted me to plan ahead.

When she arrived, we biked through Keswick and on to the west, turning left as the lake curved to the south. I saw a small marina ahead. We parked the bikes and went out to the lake. I saw kayaks, paddleboards, rowboats, powerboats, lots of versions of sailboats, and even a few large launches with official designations. And a few private boats big enough to be yachts. The place must be incredibly busy in high summer with all the boats concentrated in the cove. But this late in the season, as summer had past, there were only a few boats putting out. Elizabeth had a bag, with food and two bottled drinks. I, of course, had my trusty bag for whatever could possibly go wrong.

Near the end of one dock was a boat with a cover, which Elizabeth removed. Underneath was a nice boat, wooden with painted hull and some painted interior. Nice wood, mahogany or teak lined the rails and some parts of the interior. It was much nicer than some of the plastic blobs docked around it. I suppose it could hold four people, but it looked small to me. No cabin, just a small space behind wood doors in the bow. Big enough for two life jackets that Elizabeth pulled out. Then she stashed our bags and the folded cover inside. I watched her and would have helped with the ropes and sail but I had no idea what to do. I quickly realized it was more efficient for me to stay out of her way while she readied the boat.

We got out of the marina without any problem. I would have rowed out or borrowed a small outboard, but she used only the wind to slip out into bigger water. The wind was steady and I watched Elizabeth handle the boat with ease. It was a nice day and I saw the attraction to sailing.

"I know nothing about sailing, but I can tell you are good at it."

"It was required of us, Ian and me, that is. The Man insisted that we learn to sail. And not just sail, but excel at it. He thought it befitted a proper class of lady and gentleman as we were supposed to be. When things went well everyone was happy. But we were kids and eventually things did not go as planned. Then the Man instituted his disciplinary policy. But in a way he did me a favor, as I like to sail and used it to get away from him as much as possible. I still sail as it calms my mind.

Sailing alone requires lots of attention and concentration, yet at the same time allows me to sink into myself and nearly meditate. What, why are you looking at me like that?"

"I think that is the most I have ever heard you say at one time. Sailing does seem to be good for you."

She blushed a little and kept a small smile. "It is good for me. You should try it."

"I would need to live near a lake like this, which I do not. But I see the appeal."

"I knew you would."

"Is this your boat?"

"Sort of. The Man bought it to train us. We've kept it since, but I'm the only one that uses it. Mum likes the water OK but is not a sailor. Ian is better than me, but he has given it up since he went off to uni. It's all mine now I suppose."

"Are you going back to university once this unpleasantness is over?"

"Probably. I would have said for sure, but now I've been I didn't like it as much as I thought I would. Getting away from home was nice. I had the freedom to do things I wanted to do, the way I wanted to do them. But the basic classes I've taken were boring. I wanted the intellectual discussions, ethical debates, and radical philosophies. I guess that will come later."

"Probably not. Universities are not what they used to be."

"You've taught in America. Are they better than us?"

"As a whole, no, they are worse. Take a student, charge them twenty years worth of wages, and give them basic training to be a cog in the industrial or intelligence machine."

"God, that sounds terrible."

"It is for most students. By the time I left the system I had a hard time recommending students stay in it. I mean, it is fine for those wanting to enter a specific industry or technical trade. An intellectual desert for those looking for the traditional liberal education as you just mentioned."

"Then I suppose I won't be going over as a visiting student."

"Just check carefully. There are still some smaller schools left that you would like. But most likely you would find what you are looking for in Europe."

As we chatted I noticed how deftly Elizabeth handled the ropes and a crank that controlled the sails. The waves today were tiny and the boat cut a nice wake through them as we went back and forth toward the south. I believe she was tacking, which exhausted my sailing vocabulary. We passed a larger island, a couple of small ones, and a tiny one. The scenery was incredible, with the surrounding mountain ridges and fluffy cumulous clouds reflecting in the water, so clear you could see several feet deep.

"You see the largest island? It is St. Herberts. We will stop there on the way back for lunch. It is sort of famous as the first Christian in the area lived there."

"I assume his name was Herbert."

"You catch on quickly for an American. The island was also written about in a children's book, and was where they filmed movies about the book."

"I think I saw part of the movie. This area does look like what I remember from it."

"Most of the lake is nice. Except for the south bank, where it's marshy."

"From what I can tell we are moving south," I said.

"Yes, I wanted to go down and poke around an island and the shoreline. It's taking longer than I expected as there is a slight southeast breeze. A wind from the north today and we would have been there already. Even a stronger head wind and I could have tacked us down faster."

"I assume that means coming back will be quicker."

"We will make quite a clip if the wind doesn't change. You aren't already tired of sailing are you?"

"No, this is enjoyable. But I like knowing the ride back is available since we don't have a motor."

"We will get back just fine. Now, I'm going to teach you some simple rules and let you take the rudder." She proceeded to tell me about how to handle the boat, moving the main sail and positioning the rudder to make everything go where it was supposed to. Then she showed me how to stop by dropping the sail and tossing the anchor. It all made sense but I doubted I would retain much.

I could see the lake ending ahead. Still picturesque, as all the lakes in the District were, although I could see the marshy areas that Elizabeth had mentioned. But I was concerned as the wind died. The sail did not even flutter, and the boat slowed to a stop. I looked around as did Elizabeth.

"That is strange, usually the wind picks up on this end," she said. "But seems to have died at the moment."

I looked at the high ridge to the west. A dark shadow crested the top. Most concerning was that there were no cirrus clouds ahead of the dark mass. What was coming was hard and probably fresh from the North Sea.

"Elizabeth, trouble is coming from the west."

"I see it. No harbinger clouds and a dead calm before it. That can't be good, with the front wall moving that fast."

"I think we are about to get hit with some new wind." I saw the long grasses bending down on the ridge, from the top at first, and now reaching the bottom. Then the wind from the northwest hit us and quickly the lake turned from placid to whitecaps.

"I've never seen a storm hit so fast. I can tack us back north but we will be in the thick of it."

"I have seen these before. Maybe not the best idea to stay on the lake. Can you get us to shore nearby? This thing will pass in half an hour." I was not concerned about Elizabeth's sailing experience getting us back, but it was going to be miserable. And the wind gust would be unpredictable, a dangerous combination with waves three feet or higher.

"Yes, I can run down to those coves over there. One even has a tiny island. That will give us some shelter from the wind and we can tie the boat up until it is over."

"Great. Now make it so." I don't think she recognized the line from one of the great science fiction television shows.

Her boat skills got us to the middle cove in less than five minutes. The wind was howling and the first wave of small hail hit us. Annoying but not dangerous like the big stuff. I had seen baseball-sized hail in Oklahoma that would go through a car windshield. Near shore, I jumped out with a rope and tied us to a tree. I was concerned about running the boat fully aground as the shoreline was rocky. Elizabeth threw the anchor out the back. We got the bags out of the boat and crouched under some low trees and bushes near shore, the only shelter in sight. I did not want to be under any big trees as the lightning began flashing around us, with incredibly loud thunder. On the lake I could see sheets of rain coming fast, and so thick I could see nothing past them. I opened my bag and gave Elizabeth a rain jacket. She quickly put it on, and I put on another from the bag.

"How did you know?" she asked.

"I got caught in one of these before while hiking. They don't come often, but when they do it can be dangerous."

"You must think me an idiot for not anticipating the storm."

"Not at all. This is a rare occurrence so I'm not surprised you have not been caught in one before. But now that you have been, I'd bet you'll be prepared for the next one, even if it never happens."

"You'd be right about that."

We watched the blackout conditions worsen as the lightning popped so fast it was like paparazzi flashbulbs.

"Elizabeth, we should move back further from the lake. I'm worried abut sheet lightning hitting us."

"What's that?"

"When lightning strikes the water, it travels horizontally over the water onto shore."

Elizabeth grabbed the lunch bag as I got mine and we crawled further back into the brush. "Is this far enough?" she asked.

"Hard to tell. If we don't get electrocuted then we will know it was."

She gave me the same exasperated look as her mother once did. It was the most Olivia-like gesture I had seen from her.

About twenty minutes later the incessant lightning and monsoon rain lessened to a major thunderstorm. Ten minutes later it was off the lake and traveling southeast at a fast pace.

"I think it is time to continue north."

"Without a stop for lunch." She held up the soggy bag with lunch in it. "I believe the sandwich bread has ceased to exist."

"Oh well, when we get back to your house I'll cook us something."

"Really? I've heard you are an excellent cook. Mum, not so much."

"I can't promise it will be excellent, but it will be hot and pathogen-free."

"I'm not sure you should use that as a slogan if you open a restaurant."

"Marketing is not my strong skill. Let's go and drain the boat."

After making preparations to sail, Elizabeth set course and we went north faster than we had come down. The lake was still choppy but manageable.

CHAPTER FIFTEEN

"Why do you call Campbell the Man?" I asked, as we sailed north.

"It is something Ian and I started not long after he married mum. He was polite enough to us at first, but always uptight. We had to act just so, dress and talk to his liking, and anything related to sports had to be done his way. When we did not conform, the Man came out if nobody was around."

"That sounds ominous."

"It was for us as kids. After a day with him we usually

had bruises where no one would see them. On a few especially bad days, we ended up at the hospital to get a cast."

"He broke bones?"

"Sometimes. But I had rather not talk about it anymore."

"I'm sorry that happened to you."

She did not reply but I felt she was glad to not continue the conversation. Campbell must have been a real monster to have harmed his young stepchildren. I imagine both Elizabeth and Ian must harbor intense hatred of a man like that.

As we approached the marina, I saw a figure standing out on the farthest dock. I had an idea who it was.

"I believe your mum has come to welcome us back."

"More like to scold me."

Elizabeth slid us into the slip we had vacated earlier while Olivia came around to stand nearby with a scowl.

"Hi Olivia, what brings you down to the docks?" I asked. "Elizabeth was showing me how to sail, and to weather a storm safely. She is quite a sailor."

"Are you two alright?" Olivia asked. I knew her well enough to know she was angry and worried, but trying not to show it. And I would keep her from going after Elizabeth by redirecting her.

"We are great. We sheltered in a cove and the only thing lost was the sandwich bread. Which I'll rectify by cooking dinner. What would you like tonight?"

I was keeping an eye on Elizabeth as she took care of the boat and put everything away. She was smiling slightly as she recognized my strategy.

"Uh, whatever you would like to cook."

"Good, we should stop at the market on the way back. I have an idea for something depending on what the market has." I stepped up onto the dock beside Olivia. I surprised her by hugging her. "Elizabeth did great today and is worthy of praise," I whispered into Olivia's ear. Olivia stared at me as I stepped back. She nodded once her acceptance. Crisis averted, I thought.

I loaded the bikes onto the car and Olivia drove me to the market. It was only a few moments during which the three of us made small talk and Elizabeth told Olivia how she handled the storm. Olivia listened graciously without criticizing, and lauded Elizabeth's actions.

I had decided to make a Southern breakfast for dinner. Eggs, bacon, grits, biscuits and gravy. It was what I might have had on a camping trip and since Elizabeth and I didn't have our lunch on the island, it was the next best thing. I would make eggs scrambled with cheese and a touch of cream. Bacon, although it was the English bacon that I had to admit was better than American bacon, with leaner and wider strips. The grits were going to be Italian polenta, which were just grits with better marketing, and a little better quality. They were also made with yellow corn, which would give them a nice color. Lastly, I picked up some potatoes to make hashbrowns. Simple to make since I only had to shred them and rinse with water, but they took a long time to cook through. They were not traditionally Southern, but they were good for breakfast.

Logistics came into play quickly. Potatoes would take the longest so they had to get started first. I had Elizabeth scramble the eggs in a bowl and add cheese and cream, then put them in the refrigerator. I had Olivia start the bacon. Not because I needed it, but rather the drippings to make gravy. After grating and lightly rinsing the potatoes, and adding salt, they went into a pan with olive oil to begin cooking. I started the biscuits, an incredibly simple recipe of adding heavy cream to flour to make a thick dough. I formed biscuits and they went into the oven. I began the making the gravy from the bacon pan, adding flour then adding broth. Last I added cream and let it simmer. I boiled the polenta in broth and it was soon thick and bubbly. I added salt, and a little cream, plus cheese. Not too much because the eggs had cheese as well. Everything came together as the eggs finished cooking.

Meanwhile, Elizabeth and Olivia opened and served some wine. Not a typical Southern breakfast drink but one had to make allowances in other countries. They set up dishes and silverware on the bar as they decided that is where we would eat.

Elizabeth retold the boat trip to Olivia, and it was already becoming a funny family legend. Somehow, the food prep was both a surreal experience with the two women and also very familiar. I was living two different realities, but it was enjoyable. I had not seen Elizabeth so relaxed and getting along with Olivia, and vice versa. Soon, everything was ready at almost the same time. Possibly more luck than my time management skills. We ate and told jokes, mostly clean. Afterward Elizabeth left to go visit with friends. I think the boat adventure had livened her up and boosted her confidence. Something she could share with her friends. As she left she hugged both of us, then gave Olivia an odd stare. Olivia and I began cleaning up the kitchen, then washing and drying dishes.

"I don't know what you did or said on the sail trip, but it worked wonders for Elizabeth," Olivia said.

"I gave a tiny amount of guidance and let her be herself. She is young, but knows what she is doing. Just needs more experience."

"Thank you. I also get your message about letting her be herself. Lately I've either been distracted and not noticing her or I've been trying to run her life."

"Neither works in her case, I think. Olivia, she also told me something disturbing."

She did not respond, but looked at me with dread. She already knew what I was about to say.

"She mentioned that Campbell was sometimes physical with her and Ian. Even resulting in broken bones at least once."

"James, I really don't want to talk about this right now." Her eyes were tearing up. I had seen her cry only a few times in her life, so I knew this was disturbing to her.

"Olivia, I don't need a discussion. At least not at this time. Can you confirm that it happened, or could have happened? I need to know in order to add that to Campbell's profile."

"Yes," was all she said.

"Thank you. Now, where do you keep the good stuff? And not that wound disinfectant you call scotch."

She seemed grateful the conversation was done. At a nearby cabinet, she opened the door and asked what I wanted. I went over to stand beside her. I decided on a combination we had once shared in the distant past that I doubt she remembered. It was a mix of Irish cream liqueur and rum. Put over ice it somehow made sense. While standing there, deciding on what to drink, I realized how close we were and touching shoulders. She made no attempt to move away. I grabbed two bottles and moved away before anything happened.

"Am I not allowed to have scotch?" she asked.

"Not tonight, at least until after you have one of these. You probably won't like it, but it will be over quick."

"Sounds like our marriage."

"Ouch, that resembles reality too much."

"Sorry, that is what happens when I don't get my scotch."

"So all I had to do was keep you buzzed on scotch to hold our marriage together for 35 years?"

"Maybe a bit more."

"Did you know that Elizabeth took me to meet David?"

"What? When?"

"Not long ago. She told me about her real father, and I decided I needed to talk to him. Rule him in or out as a suspect."

"Which way did you rule? I could not see him as a suspect. He doesn't have that decisiveness in him."

"He's not a suspect. But what about me? Do I have it in me?"

"When I knew you before, no, you did not. I don't know about you now, but I would guess not."

I laughed. "Then you didn't know me then or now."

"What do you mean?"

"Not long ago a man died on my living room floor. He deserved it. I won't tell you about my teenage years in Atlanta."

"James, I'm shocked. I've never seen that side of you."

"Of course not, you only got the good side. If I had been here a few weeks ago and known what I now know, I'd have tossed Campbell off that cliff myself."

"I can't believe you said that."

"I can't believe he was your husband. Why were you separated?"

"Ian left for college. Once there, he always had reason to stay, even on holidays. One day I confronted him about not coming home. He told me about Campbell. I guess he was off at college and realizing what it meant to be out of the house. He said he only told me because he was worried about Elizabeth being home and taking the brunt of Campbell's abuse. I did not believe him at first, but he convinced me with plenty of horrific details. That night I came here and brought Elizabeth with me."

"Thank you for telling me."

We sat and Olivia had her first sip of my concoction. "You are right. I hate this."

"It takes a moment to grow on you. Let me know after the third sip."

"If I'm not retching by then I will."

"What was that look Elizabeth gave you as she was leaving? I'm not up on female-to-female unspoken communication."

"That was her giving me permission."

"Permission to do what? Oh… That's why she left."

"Got it in one. Age has made you wiser."

"In some ways. I must say I wasn't expecting that."

"Neither was I. You've made an impression."

"I hope it is a good one. She deserves it."

"That she does."

"So what do you say we punch the permission ticket?

"Romantic as always."

"Yeah, but you know I'm teasing."

"Are you?"

"I am. Are you?"

"I suppose so. I can't see much good from us getting entangled."

"No, it would not solve anything, and only add to our confusing relationship."

"I agree. I'm also finding this obnoxious drink getting better."

"Told you."

"What is next with your investigation?"

"I need you to take me to Campbell's place of business."

"Why? It's just an office and a warehouse."

"Possibly, but I believe Campbell was doing something illegal there, along with his regular business."

"You must be mistaken. I know he was not a good man, but I don't think he would risk his business for anything. He inherited it, and it was his prize possession."

"Still, humor me. I have my reasons."

"I'll take you there tomorrow."

CHAPTER SIXTEEN

Olivia drove us toward Manchester. Campbell's office and operations were about a two-hour drive south. We talked about nothing much on the way, until we got closer. I needed more information about her recent husband.

"How often did you see Campbell the last few years?" I asked.

"Not often. We went to a few social events and work events. I think everyone knew we were separated but we kept up the pretense."

"Family holidays?"

"No, otherwise the children would not have attended. Campbell complained and threatened to cut off their college tuition. He never did as he knew that would have been seen as petty. I think he also believed that by paying for college he kept some control."

"Or kept them quiet."

"That too."

"Did he have any close family?"

"No, his parents are deceased and he had little contact with his siblings."

"Was that his decision or theirs?"

"Theirs. They did not much like him. Lately I've wondered if when he was younger he terrorized them."

"It is possible. Certain personalities display that trait even when young. You said Campbell was in the chemical business."

"Yes, he sourced, bought and supplied quite a few operations in the UK and the continent. He also had a small manufacturing facility set up next to the warehouse. We will see both today."

"Where did Campbell mostly do business?"

"When not in the office he tended to be in London much of the time. There he handled the local and continental customers. Lots of social activity and some political interests. He also had overseas trips to Bangkok and Moscow."

Bangkok? That brought up possibilities. Drugs, gem smuggling, and prostitution. From the chemistry perspective, drugs seemed more likely. Business in Moscow could be nearly anything illegal. Smuggling technology, money laundering, drugs, or dozens of options. "Those are two unusual destinations for a chemical supplier."

"I suppose. He never said what he did on those trips."

"Where in Europe did he go?"

"Mostly the Netherlands and Belgium." The two countries with the most drug manufacturing in Europe.

She pulled in front of a building located in a commercial park near Runcorn. It was between Liverpool and Manchester. A sedate car park with landscaped trees by the road and nice bushes near the building, with a small manicured lawn split by a walkway to a glass door. Logistically, it had access to a major highway, the railroad, and a canal with docks. All good infrastructure for a business requiring imports and exports of chemicals, from bulky powders to tankers of liquids. But the building was not huge, nor did I see outside tanks and bins.

"Olivia, I wasn't sure what it would look like, but I wasn't expecting this. Chemical plants in the US are larger and much uglier."

"The business used to be on the other side of the river, in a larger space with land covered with storage tanks. I imagine it was more to your expectations. It was abandoned due to pollution. He moved it here and made it smaller, specializing in smaller quantities of more expensive chemicals."

There was a keypad, call button, and speaker by the door. Olivia punched in a code and the door unlocked.

"Ah, I guess he didn't change the code after all. I thought he would have."

"Maybe he wanted to know if or when you came to visit."

"I doubt it since I have not been here in two years."

Inside there was a hallway with nice carpet and an alcove with plants, and a glass partition with a reception desk behind it. No one was there as we walked past it to another door. Olivia entered a code, and it opened to reveal an office area with cubicles and six glass doors on the peripheral walls. About half were occupied. Typical younger professionals on the phone or computer generating a light buzz of noise that diminished once they noticed Olivia.

Two women and a man got up to offer Olivia condolences. The man asked Olivia about Campbell's personal things in his office. I realized he must be the man in charge when Campbell was gone. Olivia introduced him to me as the Vice-President of the company, Owen Martell. She told him we wanted to go through Campbell's office then walk through the plant. Owen offered to give us the tour when we were ready, then Olivia led me to the office behind one of the glass doors.

Campbell's office was about what I expected. Wood desk and credenza behind it, leather chair, and darker green walls with photographs of him in various poses. A pheasant hunt, a sailing yacht, on a horse, on a river fly fishing, and in an ornate bar with other men smoking cigars. There was one family photograph with the four of them dressed formally and no one smiling. I closed the door behind us and immediately began looking through the credenza. I stopped when I saw Olivia standing by the door with a vacant stare. She had not moved or spoken since we came in.

"Olivia, can you give me a few minutes to look through the office? Then we can get out of here."

She nodded yes. I went back to the credenza and found absolutely nothing. A few office supplies of pens, pencils, and staples, but not a scrap of paper anywhere. I checked the desk and found the same. Whoever had searched Campbell's home office had done the same here. I opened a few pens and the stapler but found no cryptic notes. It was time to leave and get Olivia out of here. She was still standing with a blank look.

"Olivia, do you want to take the picture with you?"

"God no. Please just put it in the trash."

Back in the office area we met Owen to give us a quick tour. The attached warehouse building was large and neatly kept. It was also climate-controlled. Different compartments held pallets of barrels, bags, or large plastic totes. We went through quickly, so I didn't get any details on what they held. Owen was rushing us, but considering Olivia's state I did not care. On the far side, we went into a wide hallway with large doors on either end, suitable for forklift traffic. It was a separate building and Owen opened the far doors but we did not go in.

"This is the manufacturing area," Owen said. "Blending liquids or powders in separate areas, plus packaging the products in everything from one kilogram bags to tanker loads. We won't go in for safety reasons."

We returned to the office area without Olivia saying anything. I asked Owen if he or others had begun cleaning out Campbell's office. He replied no, they would leave it for Olivia or her representative. I thanked him at the door and took Olivia back to the car.

"Olivia, would you like me to drive?"

She laughed. "Not at all. You would kill us deader than Campbell in the first mile."

"At least you have your sense of humor back."

"That, plus my sense of self-preservation. I'll drive."

"Olivia, can we stop at Castlerigg when we get back? I'd like to walk around outside a few minutes." Castlerigg was just outside Keswick and was a green pasture with an ancient standing stone ring. A good place to clear my head after four hours in the car and going through Campbell's office.

"Yes, I'll stop. It will be good to air out my head a few minutes. Unless you are planning on touching a stone and transporting back to America."

"I wish. But that only happens on television. But I do wonder how many people wander around touching stones these days, wanting to go somewhere else or travel to another time."

"Just about everyone does, James. But it doesn't happen, does it?"

"No, at least no one I know about has done it. You are still upset about being in Campbell's office."

"No, not being in his office exactly. Seeing that horrible family picture is what did it."

"Why, did something happen on that day?"

"No. But something happened our entire marriage. And I didn't even know about it until later. I went on my business trips and he harmed my children. That makes me complicit in his crimes."

"I don't think that is how it works, Olivia. You can't blame yourself for everything he did."

"Yes, I can. And I will for the rest of my life."

I struggled to come up with a logical argument in reply to her. But I realized anything I said would be wrong. Olivia wasn't grieving Campbell, she was grieving her relationship with her children.

I was not sure how to console her without sounding trite or condescending. She needed her time to process everything, and it would likely take years. We stopped for tea on the way back, but she was still quiet. Walking around Castlerigg finally broke Olivia's mood.

"Thank you for coming over James. It has been good to have someone around."

"You are welcome. You will need to start talking through this with Ian and Elizabeth."

"I will. I feel like I failed my children."

"Take your time with that. But what is important now is to be there for them. You have the rest of your life to do so, but now is a good time to start."

"What do you think happened to Campbell?"

"I'm not sure yet."

"Are you protecting me from what you know or suspect?"

"I need to check on a few things before I tell you what I think happened."

"Will you protect my children?"

"Always, Olivia. But I want to talk to Ian."

"Please don't. He does not need to be involved in this."

I nodded agreement but already knew I would. Olivia did not know he was already involved. Or maybe she did.

At the Inn I made a call. It was late in America but I wanted another perspective.

"Hi Donna. Sorry it is so late."

"James, good to hear from you. I was up anyway because of too much tea. Been trying to bulldoze through a messy plot sequence."

"Bulldozing through a romance seems harsh."

"But necessary. This one should have been easy, but my characters keep going off on tangents and misbehaving. How is it going there?"

"Sort of the same. I'm chasing tangents and people are misbehaving."

"Of course they are. They are human after all."

"I feel like I am in a slow-motion free fall, dropping through layers of gauzy half-truths, lies of omission, and outright deception. And all that on top of working in a legal system I don't understand, in a country where I don't know all the customs as I pursue who might have killed a man. Or maybe it was an accident."

"Who is doing the lying or omitting?"

"Mostly the person I'm supposed to be helping."

"Then she is hiding something. Maybe not the murder, but something important to her. Maybe she knows the murderer, or has a secret she can't afford to let you find. Again, all human traits are similar that are frustrating but understandable if frustrating."

"I've thought the same thing. But it complicates every-thing unnecessarily. I could care less about family secrets or financial skullduggery. But I'm close to finding what she's hiding, or thinks she's hiding."

"You'll have to convince her to trust you or go around her to finish up."

"I'm doing both. Without other resources it's the best chance I have."

"Maybe you need other resources."

"I wish. But maybe I have something I can try. Millard's OctoPosse came through with some information that could help."

"OctoPosse? Do you fancy yourself on a James Bond adventure?"

"I hope not. I needed something to call his group and that was the best I came up with."

"Do they know you call them that?"

"Not yet. I thought I'd have them over for dinner and give them T-shirts with the logo."

"Not your best idea. I'd go with hats instead since most are bald."

"Thanks for talking tonight."

"No problem. See you soon?"

"I think so. No more than a few days."

"Goodnight."

"Bye Donna."

CHAPTER SEVENTEEN

The bus ride to Penrith was pleasant. Buses in the area were clean, generally on time, and had large windows for viewing the stunning countryside. This was my second trip to Penrith in a few days, but today I was only there to catch a train. Two hours later, I was in Glasgow. A town that somehow I had never been to before, despite having been close to it several times. I was disappointed I would be there such a short time and not get to see the city. But I had a single purpose: to talk to Ian, and then I would leave. To really get to know a city, even superficially, takes about five days. I had closer to two hours.

I knew Olivia did not want me to talk to him. But Elizabeth had no such prohibition, and she helped set up the visit. I was going to meet him between classes near the university campus in a small cafe. Neutral ground and no interference with his classes, so when Olivia found out she could not be too mad. That was my thought but I knew she'd be furious. Apparently I did that a lot and nothing bad had happened so no harm in continuing my work.

I got off the train at the central station, then hired a car to take me around the university so I could at least see some of it on my abbreviated trip. From what I could tell through the car window it seemed nice. But I had rather been out and walking for at least two days to have gotten a feel for it.

Then on to the cafe for the meeting. It was an old building but inside was a fresh coffee shop and cafe with wood plank flooring, metal tables, and a high exposed ceiling. In the back were upholstered chairs and loveseats with low tables between. Busy in the front with a mix of college students and professionals and quiet in the back for the online crowd.

I saw someone familiar from family photographs I'd seen. He was sitting near the back. He stood when he noticed me, so Elizabeth must have sent him my picture.

"Hello, you must be Ian," I said.

"And you are James Wilder, rather Dr. Wilder."

"Yes, but no one calls me that as I don't use it anymore. James is fine."

"You are the American that nearly became my parent."

"Yeah, I really dodged one there." I knew he was teasing so I hit it back over the net. His smirk dropped.

"A quick one. Unlike dear old stodgy Campbell."

"Obviously I didn't know him, but I am glad you see the difference."

"You must have heard he was not a nice person."

"From more than one person, in regard to more than one characteristic."

"You are direct and don't mince around."

"No reason to. He is no longer around and now I'd like to find out more about him and more importantly, what happened to him."

"I can't help you."

"Maybe I should explain why I'm doing this."

"Please proceed but I don't have much to say about any of this."

"Olivia asked me to come over to help exonerate her as she is a person of interest. You know that already. Since I've been here I have modified that aim. The information I've gathered leads me to say, bluntly, is that Campbell's death, whether intentional or accidental, was well-deserved. Anyone that he hurt, if in anyway involved, should be protected. The more I discover then the better case I can build to provide that protection, if needed."

"That was a lot of words chasing around a theme you are taking pains not to say."

"I can be much more direct."

"Elizabeth told me you are alright and I can trust you. But then that is how you would position yourself if you were trying to get into her good graces and trick her into giving away information. Same as you are doing with me."

"That is exactly what I would do, if I was good at subterfuge and acting. I'm pretty good at the first but not the second. Had you spent much time around me you would find out. But my motivation is as I stated."

"I think it's time for you to be more direct."

"Honestly, I can't tell if Olivia believes you and Elizabeth had nothing to do with Campbell's death and wants me to prove it, or whether she believes one or both of you did it and wants me to ferret it out so she will know how best to cover it up."

"See, direct is more your style. What is your role if you discover either Elizabeth or me was involved? Will you turn us in?"

"No, I won't. I'll give everything I find to Olivia. I know she will do everything she can to protect you both. I'll go over strategies with her if she lets me, then I go home."

"Just like that, you will leave it alone?"

"Yes, I will. I'm doing this as a favor to Olivia. I'm not here to ruin your or Elizabeth's lives. Just the opposite. Then again, I have no direct evidence that either of you were involved. But if so, better I find out than the authorities."

"I would like to take a break and get more tea to think about it. What would you like?"

"Breakfast tea if they have a good blend."

"It is excellent here. I'll get us a pot. Cream or lemon?"

"Just sugar."

Ian was gone a few moments. I kept an eye on him in

case he skipped out the front door. But he brought back the tea and we fixed our cups.

"James, I am curious. You are inferring that Elizabeth, me, or both of us could be involved with the death of our stepfather. Why do you think that?"

"Because I saw the footage from the Penrith train station the night of his death."

"Ah, that would lead you to that conclusion."

"That and other clues."

"Did anyone else see the footage?"

"No I managed to be the only one to view it."

"That is great. One less thing to worry about."

"Elizabeth also mentioned the Man and gave a very brief explanation of that term. But enough to know he was a monster."

"He wanted to be. But only to us. Because we were defenseless when mum was gone, and because of his standing no one would believe us if we told. Classic abuser behavior. Something I've learned here at university."

"Good reason to have him gone."

"Yes. Did you find anything else? We always believed he had another secret family or was involved in insider trading. Something petty but illegal."

"I did actually."

"Really? Can you tell me?"

"No one else knows any details, although I mentioned to Olivia he might have been involved in illegal activities. I'll tell her more if she needs to prepare a defense or provide an alternate motive for his death. But you and Elizabeth should know. Campbell was almost certainly a major player in providing chemicals to the methamphetamine manufacturers in Europe."

"How did you find out? We knew he was bad, but I would not have guessed that."

"It is what I do, and to be honest, I got lucky. It is what separates good and bad investigators. The random blessing of luck."

"Interesting. The old dog was shady."

"He was, and another avenue to explore. It is likely someone in that business wanted him dead."

"And you aren't going to the police?"

"No, once again it will go to Olivia to do with it whatever is required to keep all of you safe. Now, is that enough to convince you to tell me your story?"

"I think so. But you must promise me to protect Elizabeth. I know you said you would, but I want to hear it directly from you."

"Ian, I promise to protect Elizabeth any way that I can. Even if she was involved, I'll do what I can to shield her and keep her safe."

"Thank you. I'll tell you what I know. Then you can decide what you need to do to fulfill your promise."

"Thank you."

"Campbell was, as Elizabeth must have told you, not a nice man. He was very particular in what he did, and what we must do to avoid his anger. Not win his affection, mind you, but to keep his displeasure at bay. When mum or anyone else was around his displeasure was manifested in some verbal abuse and our being sent away from his presence. Which was fine with us of course. He knew that, so when he had us alone, especially for a few days, he let loose the Man. We might be walking on the trail, me and Elizabeth, cutting up as we walked. Then he would punch one of us very hard in the middle of the back and knock us down. As we got older, most of his punches were on me, and never the face. But he threatened to hit Elizabeth to keep me in line, then often would hit me anyway."

"A stupid brute. Elizabeth mentioned he broke bones."

"Yes. The worst time was when we were hiking near the spot where his body was found. Elizabeth was not minding him, then finally spouted off at him. He grabbed her, then his face sort of lost all expression. That is when we knew the Man was coming out. He stood there holding her a few seconds with one hand on her arm, staring at nothing. Then he wrapped his hands around her lower arm and broke it. She screamed of course, and we walked back to the car. While she was sobbing other people on the trail were being told by Campbell she had fallen and hurt her arm. We got back to the car and he drove us home. Would not take her to the hospital until the next morning. We were warned worse would happen if we told anyone."

"That is horrible. Where was Olivia during all this?"

"Away on a business trip for the week. He told her the same story, that Elizabeth had fallen on the hike. There was always a story to explain an injury. A warning to never tell anyone. And a promise that if we told mum he would do even worse to her. Because mum was gone only a few times a year, we were able to survive."

"Something I normally would not say, but it seems he was a man worth killing. At least sending to jail for 20 years."

"You can imagine how relieved I felt at being able to

escape and go to school. At the same time, I was so worried for Elizabeth. But she was old enough and physical enough that he seemed to leave her alone. Still, I worried. At first break I came home from uni and told mum everything in detail."

"What was her reaction?"

"Disbelief at first. But I had meticulously recorded every incident. She soon believed me then confronted him in a rage. He denied everything. But she and Elizabeth moved to Keswick immediately."

"Good for her. At least she believed you. I've known some people that would not have."

"She did. I felt great relief since Elizabeth was out of his immediate reach. I thought there would have been a divorce, legal action against him, or something, but mum did not pursue it. After two years, Elizabeth came to me and we decided to confront him. She needed closure and a chance to scream at him, I think."

"I assume that was recently."

"Yes, the night he died."

"What happened that night on the ridge? I know you were both there from the tape."

"It is a little complicated. We needed to get him there, but without knowing Elizabeth would be present. Neither of us had a car, so I came down and she came up by train, as you saw. I met him on the pretense of having dinner and a hike. I talked to him a few times in the weeks previous since it was part of our plan; me keeping contact with him some so when I suggested a hike he would not suspect anything. He let me drive us to the car park by the ridge to take a sunset hike. Elizabeth hired a car and was already on the trail. She would wait for us at the top. It was his favorite trail and the place where he broke her arm. He and I ascended the ridge and walked the trail as the sun set. Elizabeth was sitting on a rock. It surprised him, since she would have nothing to do with him."

"I suppose things went badly when she confronted him."

"Definitely. But we thought it could, so she was ready. Anyway, she recounted his misdeeds, gradually getting louder. He argued back, his face getting redder by the minute. I let her yell and kept my attention on him. When his face went slack and he moved toward her I grabbed his arm. He's a big guy, and he spun around and pushed me, and I tripped and fell back. He went back after Elizabeth, but she was ready. She had extended her baton and thwacked him across his forearm. Sounded like a cricket bat hitting a tire. He took another step and she did the same to his knee. He dropped to the ground and sat there. He looked a little confused which was odd. I got up and Elizabeth and I left to go back to the car. After a few minutes of walking she left and went back to where he was. She said she wanted to check on him in case he couldn't walk. I told her not to worry, he could always call out on his phone, or even sit there all night since it wasn't cold. But she insisted."

"She went back to him, alone? How long was she gone?"

"Not long. She came back and said he was not there. He must have gotten up and kept walking. We walked down to the car, and decided to take it over to the next car park. It was our last chance to be petty to him, so he would have to go find his car. Then we called for a car and went back to the station. She went back to her dorm in Manchester and I back to my apartment in Glasgow."

"Then you heard about his death."

"Yes, and I must say that I assumed the worst. Somehow Elizabeth got him off that cliff."

"Did she?"

"She denied it. But she was distraught. She said she must have caused him to jump after we left, and it was almost as bad as killing him."

"Do you think it possible she killed him?"

"I think it possible because she was so mad. But no, I don't think she did. But you must protect her, because of the slight chance she did. Or because she really might have caused him to jump."

"Do you think he would kill himself?"

"Honestly, no I do not."

"From what little I know, I don't think so either. But then I don't see Elizabeth having the mentality to do it either, nor being physical enough to throw him off the cliff."

"I've thought the same, but can't come up with a reasonable explanation. What do you think happened?"

"I don't know. Which tells me I don't have all the information yet. Something else was happening on the ridge, and I need to ferret out some more secrets."

"I wish you luck with that. I know Elizabeth would be grateful if you determined what happened as well."

"Thank you Ian. I think I have what I need to start wrapping this up. Even if I don't find the truth, I believe Elizabeth is innocent. I hope you will be available to support her and convince her it is not her fault."

"I intend to. Are you going to tell mum?"

"I may have to, if for no other reason than for her to also support Elizabeth."

"Thank you for what you are doing James. It was nice to meet you."

"You too, Ian."

CHAPTER EIGHTEEN

I had to assume Ian was telling the truth. I detected no lies, but he cared about Elizabeth and might have been protecting her. But assuming it was truth, then there was another party involved. Considering the type of people Campbell was doing business with, an unhappy drug dealer or manufacturer was the likely culprit. My last thought, though, was much darker. If Campbell had told Olivia about his hike with Ian, possibly she was on the ridge that night. She had motivation and no alibi. Then I wondered whether Campbell's home office and place of business were so empty of anything useful because Olivia had cleaned them out.

I hated that two of three suspects were people I knew and cared for. Well, I cared for Elizabeth and used to care for Olivia. I very much needed to prove someone else was responsible for Campbell's death. I walked up to see Olivia at her house. Good timing as the tea was just ready.

"Olivia, anything the authorities have is closed to me. Do you have connections or any way to get information they may have?"

"No, my lawyer has given me everything that has been released. I don't know anyone on the police side that could be helpful. Why?"

"I do not have much to work with so far, and I believe I have exhausted my avenues of investigation."

"Do you have any suspects?"

"Sort of, but nothing concrete. Now a new motive has come to light. Did you know Campbell was involved with supplying chemicals to illegal methamphetamine manufacturers?"

"No, I had no idea. Did he really do that? Was that what you meant by he was doing something illegal?"

"I'm confident he was involved with it. Are you sure there was nothing odd you knew or heard about? There must have been some clues, or evidence of stress on his part."

"He was stressed the few times we talked. Even mundane topics like the children's tuition set him off."

"Nothing else?"

"He was doing some things I thought were odd," Olivia

said. "Before I left Macclesfield and came here, he set up a bitcoin account for his business."

"Bitcoin? Odd for a regular businessman. But it has been used for moving money for illegal purposes. Using it to take payment for supplying restricted chemicals makes sense."

"I don't know anymore than that."

"Would the other people at his office know anything?"

"I doubt it. I've known Owen for years, and he could not keep a secret nor would he do anything illegal."

"But someone there must have been involved. Someone mixing the chemicals, or arranging transport."

"I understand what you are saying, I just don't know who it might be. Or he could have let in someone after hours that did those jobs."

"That is possible if he wanted to keep his secrets. Having regular employees involved would have been a liability."

"Who is on your short list of suspects?"

"Of the current suspects, I believe you know most of them. But then, you had me over for this very reason, knowing I'd have this list. My role is to help you refine your story and to find weaknesses in it so you could better defend yourself. And if not you, then to do the same for the other two suspects, Elizabeth and Ian. You thought if I found out, whether you or the children were involved, then not only would I keep quiet I'd help you hide it."

"All that is true. But I also had another ulterior motive. I wanted you to get to know Elizabeth. She needed to know there were still decent men, unlike Campbell."

"Possibly, but that would only make me want to protect her more."

She said nothing; she didn't have to speak. We both knew the truth. Honestly, I disliked Olivia's motives as they were self-serving as ever. But having a connection with Elizabeth was more important than the manipulation behind it. Yet it did not help me find the murderer.

I was at a standstill in what I could do. I needed more information on Campbell Stewart but didn't know how to get it. I had no contacts with the local police or judges and did not think I could persuade them in a couple of days to start sharing with me. Then I had a thought. It could uncover something, or go nowhere. Someone I previously worked with in the Netherlands once mentioned a member of his family worked at Interpol. A long shot but it was all I had.

I called my former associate, Peter. He answered and was surprised to hear from me. We caught up a few moments and traded news about the industry and people we knew. The list of people kept getting shorter as people retired or died. I finally got to the point.

"Peter, I remember you once mentioned you had a family member working at Interpol."

"True, my brother-in-law Jan has worked there for many years. Why do you ask?"

"It is a long story, but I am in Britain helping out an old acquaintance. Her husband recently died, and I just discovered he was probably supplying chemicals to methamphetamine manufacturers in Europe. He owned a chemical supply company so he had opportunity to make and transport the chemicals."

"That is alarming. Do the local authorities know?"

"Not yet, but they will. I thought of Interpol since it seems most of the chemicals were shipping to the Netherlands and Belgium."

"Ah, I see your concern. Just a moment while I look at my phone and find his contact information."

"Sure, I'll wait."

"Yes, I have it. His name is Jan, and I'll text you the contact card."

"Thank you, Peter. I'll give him a call to let him know."

Before I called Jan I needed to have my story straight. I was a friend of the family, investigating an untimely death. I found evidence that the deceased, owner of a chemical supply company, was making and delivering methamphetamine precursors to the Netherlands and Belgium. Could he check and determine whether true? If so, then he or I could alert the UK or EU authorities, as appropriate.

I made the call and gave him the brief background information I had already rehearsed.

"What is the name of the individual?" he asked.

"Campbell Stewart. I have a home address and a business name and address, which is where I believe the chemicals originated."

"Yes, please give me those."

I did and waited as he reviewed the information.

"Dr. Wilder, what specific evidence can you provide that this man was involved in illegal activities?"

"Beyond what I've already said, he had a bitcoin account."

"Do you have the information so I can check that?"

"No, I don't."

"Dr. Wilder, you have provided vague information about a deceased individual. There may be something to your concerns, but there likely is not. Frankly, I'm not sure I have enough to even make an inquiry. We normally have more evidence before conducting any investigation. If the man were still alive I would not even proceed due to privacy issues. As you know, chemicals can be used for other purposes than illegal drug manufacturing."

"Thank you for listening."

"If this even moves forward, which I won't promise, I am not authorized to provide any information back to you. I hope you understand."

"What about notifying his widow?"

"Are you her legal representative?"

"No, but I can provide her legal representative."

"Again, most irregular. I doubt there is any reason for us to contact her. I assume there is nothing else."

"No."

"Then good day Dr. Wilder."

The call was completely unsatisfactory. Before I called I was not sure how it might develop, but I did not envision it going that poorly. Now, even if they found something I would not know the outcome. Short of documents from his business or a confession from one of his collaborators, I was not going to have anything to pursue on an alternative suspect. That just left Olivia and Elizabeth on the list.

I thought of other options. Perhaps Olivia could have a forensic accounting of Campbell's assets to look for unexplained income. Or a detailed accounting of business' inventory to look for unexplained missing chemicals or odd shipment manifests. The same type of documents

Millard had told me about and forwarded. But those two strategies would take weeks if not months. I would suggest it to Olivia and then go home. I had nothing further to investigate or contribute.

I received a text from Olivia. She asked if I wanted to walk along the river trail near Keswick. I texted her back that would be fine. She picked me up from the Inn and we parked near the river. The walk here, like everywhere in the District was pleasant and scenic.

"James, if something were to happen to me, would you keep an eye on Elizabeth?"

"Of course I would."

"She's a legal adult, the estate would take care of her needs, and even though I've distanced myself from family, she has aunts and uncles to see to her. But I'd feel better knowing you were in her life. I know it's asking a lot since you are going back to America."

"Even if you had not asked I would have done so, Olivia. Well, as much as she would let me. What about Ian?"

"He's well along into adulthood, and after graduating university next year he already has a career lined up. I'm more worried about Elizabeth, as she has not as much structure in her life yet."

"I will look after her. But I don't think there is any chance you will go away for Campbell's death."

"Thank you just the same, James."

I thought about my time spent with Olivia and those around her. Meeting Elizabeth, Ian, and even her second husband David had given me insights about who Olivia was, based on their interactions with her.

For the first time, I recognized and admired Olivia for who she was, not for who I thought she was, or who I wanted her to be. That realization freed me from any attraction or ill thought toward her. I finally saw that we should not have been together, something she had known long ago. The old resentment and frustrations dropped away. Maybe this was part of the mystery I was meant to solve.

As we approached her car, I noticed a black sedan parked beside it. A minute later, a man in a nondescript suit got out and waited for us. He was average size with sharp eyes. I initially felt a twinge of unease, wondering if Campbell's drug clientele had caught up to us. But the car and the man seemed more official. He was still threatening, but in a different way. His voice matched his eyes.

"Good day. I'm Detective Chief Superintendent Fordham, with the Cumbria Constabulary and a joint appointment in the National Crime Agency and one other organization to remain nameless. I use DCS Fordham as my identifier."

"I recognize you from the Penrith office, but we have not met," Olivia said.

"You are correct. I would like a word with you both. It may take a few minutes. Perhaps you would be kind enough to follow me to the department?"

"Is that a request or an official demand?" I asked.

He smiled but did not reply.

"That would be fine, DCS Fordham," Olivia said.

CHAPTER NINETEEN

The ride to the department was tense. Olivia was afraid they knew something and Elizabeth was in trouble. I tried to convince her not to jump to that conclusion. And deny everything to DCS Fordham.

"Doctor Stewart and Doctor Wilder." DCS Fordham shook hands with both of us, then we all sat. "Thank you both for coming. Although had you not agreed I would have insisted, as you surmised, Dr. Wilder. Now, as I understand it, Dr. Stewart, you have asked Dr. Wilder here to act as a representative to informally investigate your husband's death."

"That is correct."

"What say you, Dr. Wilder?"

"It is true."

"Thank you. I had to get both of you to confirm that verbally to continue this conversation. Dr. Stewart, do I have your permission to present our findings in the presence of Dr. Wilder?" I wasn't sure where this was going, but my usually reliable gut was telling me this was going to be unpleasant.

"Yes, whatever you are prepared to share with me, he is welcome to stay and hear it," Olivia said.

"Good. In a moment you will understand the seriousness of the situation. I hope that leads you to decide to choose the right course. Exercising the good judgement I believe you to have."

"I'll try."

"I was at first concerned with your prior relationship with Dr. Wilder. A civil union lasting approximately twenty-five months. That caused us to investigate Dr. Wilder. But he was not in the country at the time of your husband's death, and has been cleared accordingly."

"Thanks, I guess," I said.

"Dr. Stewart, were you aware your husband, through his company, was laundering money and procuring supplies for Russian illegal drug interests?"

"Not at all. Are you sure?"

He looked at me. "Dr. Stewart, I believe Dr. Wilder has already informed you that he suspected your husband was selling chemicals to methamphetamine operations in Europe."

"Oh, yes, he did tell me. But I did not know they were Russian, nor that he was laundering money."

"Thank you for clarifying those specifics," he said somewhat sarcastically. "Now we are caught up then. But yes, we are quite sure of his illegal activities. After his death, we were prepared to let things simmer down and quietly dismantle your husband's business. His death seemed to end our investigations into certain aspects of financial impropriety, drug manufacture, and other possible crimes. Had we continued, that would have left you at a financial disadvantage, I'm afraid, Dr. Stewart. But Dr. Wilder's inquiry at Interpol has pushed us to reconsider other options. Options, frankly, we should have already recognized."

"What options?"

"Dr. Stewart, you are currently unemployed. I would like you to consider taking over your husband's company."

"What? I don't understand what this is about."

"We feel that the Russians ended their business relationship with your husband because he was supplying their competitors, and they ended his life over the dispute. The Interpol inquiry, which we know they monitor, may have scared them off for a bit, but it also added some legitimacy to the farce of investigating you for murder. Of course, we have known all along you did not do it, but we needed to keep up appearances. We have a new opportunity. The chemicals your husband provided are difficult to source otherwise. We believe if Dr. Wilder ceases all inquiries and leaves the country, while you take over the business, they will contact you to continue operations. When that happens we will be able to monitor and infiltrate their operation."

"You believe the Russians killed Campbell?" I asked.

"Yes, they have a knack for encouraging people to fall from lethal heights."

"I don't know anything about his business," Olivia said.

"You don't need to. Manage people and take care of budgets is all you have to do. I know your background is adequate to pick up the technical details. You will also have access to our experts at any time. We intend to place one of ours inside the office anyway to ensure your security."

"I don't know, it does not seem right somehow. I'm not sure I'm the right person."

"Dr. Stewart, if you decide against this, we will shut down the business and take almost all the assets. If you cooperate, then the business will continue. What that means for you is the business is no longer liable for seizure unless you conduct illegal activities outside our purview. After our operation is concluded you will be free to continue the business, sell it, or shut it down and liquidate it."

"Will you be able to keep her safe?" I asked.

"Yes, we will have surveillance on Dr. Stewart at all times. A team of four will be assigned to her for 24 hour coverage. Her children as well."

"I'll do it," she said.

I thought she answered too quickly. But I understood her reasoning. If these guys thought the Russians killed her husband, and she acted accordingly, then no one would look elsewhere.

"Thank you. We now need to finalize the legal framework. Please have your solicitor available to discuss details. As for you, Dr. Wilder, your assistance in this matter is nearly concluded. We need a signed statement that this meeting and discussion will be kept confidential. The other requirement is that you leave the country. We explained your inquiry to Interpol, portraying you as a writer with no official connection to the family or law enforcement. You were looking for a story but there was none. Luckily Interpol recognized an active investigation and notified us."

"Am I expelled forever?"

"I don't think that is necessary. A year or two should do. I would advise the longer term. You will have my card so I suggest you contact me before making travel plans to the UK. Oh, and Dr. Wilder?"

"Yes?"

"Please know you've placed attention on yourself from some unsavory people that may or may not make contact. If they do, and you survive, please contact me."

"I appreciate the warning. Any estimates of that likelihood?"

"Were you to stay here as Dr. Stewart took over the business, I would estimate fifty percent. That could also jeopardize the entire operation and Dr. Stewart's livelihood. The sooner you leave the faster that decreases."

"That seems like my exit song."

"What they say in America—don't let the door hit you on the way out. I'll give you two an opportunity to say your goodbyes. Then I'll take you to the airport Dr. Wilder." He left the room.

"Olivia, you may not want to do this."

"I really don't. But I feel I have no choice."

"You probably don't. But it gets attention away from other areas that you want to remain quiet."

"I was thinking that as well. It seems to be the best all-around solution."

"I think so too. I suppose I'll get back to the Clareridge and pack."

"James, I have no words sufficient to thank you. Whatever happens, you saved my sanity."

"Don't thank me too quickly. You still have issues that require attention and utmost care. I hope you and your children find whatever healing is needed."

"We will, over time. Thank you again James."

"You are welcome."

DCS Fordham came back in. "Olivia, if you would be kind enough to stay a short while. We took the liberty to call your solicitor and he will be here in a few minutes. My associates will give you both the details. Then you will have a working agreement that both you and your lawyer can scrutinize. We hope to finalize it rather quickly."

"Now James, we also took the liberty of booking you a ticket from Manchester to Atlanta. Your flight leaves in a few hours. I'll come with you to the airport. We'll drop by the Clareridge and pick up your things."

"I'll go, but with one condition."

"I don't think you are in a position to demand conditions."

"In this case it's a very easy one, and on the way."

"Let's talk in the car. Goodbye Olivia, I'm sure we will be talking the next few days. James, let's go."

"Goodbye and good luck, Olivia."

"Goodbye James. Thank you so much for coming over."

Then we were done. On the way to the car, I got the feeling I might never see her again.

The driver was familiar. The same person I'd seen a few times.

"I believe you know our driver," DCS Fordham said. "He shall remain nameless as you don't need to know."

"I've seen him around."

"Yes, he's been keeping an eye on you. It was not an undercover operation so he did not need to surveil you incognito."

"You wanted me to know someone was tailing me?"

"In a way."

"Oh, you wanted someone else to know you were tailing me."

"Exactly. It suited our purpose in this matter. More so that the other side would think we were incompetent."

"It would appear this is a complicated game."

"Always is. The better the criminal the better we need to play."

"I'm glad I could play a small role."

"You have been most helpful, more than you know."

"Then my fast exit must also play a part in your scheme."

"Very much so. We do certain things in an obvious way so the other side does not see the other things we need to keep hidden. Oh, what prompted you to suspect Mr. Stewart was involved in the drug trade?"

"His stapler."

"Please explain."

"In his home office, in the stapler, underneath the

staples. A tiny note with two precursors and tartaric acid, three important chemicals for making meth in the EU. Plus numbers but I did not know what they meant."

I saw him look at the driver, who was looking back at him in the rear view mirror. An unsaid message was being passed.

"I put the note back exactly where I found it. I wasn't sure whether it was missed during the search or had been planted."

"It will be handled, don't worry about it."

"It has occurred to me that, considering your profession, everything you've said to me could be lies. Perhaps the night on the ridge went differently than you've said. But it was the best story to get me to leave quickly and quietly.

"I understand your perspective. I will try to rephrase in a different way. Do my lies, or alleged lies, match your observed facts?

I had to think a minute. "I think things match up well."

"Then you should consider it the most likely truth. Or I'm the most accomplished spy in the world and all this is a masterful manipulation of multiple people for no good reason."

"I see your point. Was our driver the same person on the ridge that night watching Campbell?"

"You are correct."

"If Elizabeth had come upon the flinging of Campbell, I assume the Russians would have eliminated her. Would your man have intervened?"

"I would have advised against it. But let's ask him."

"Had she reappeared at an inopportune time, I would

have acted as the drug addict I was disguised as and gone yelling at them," the driver said. "With their attention on me I'd expect her to run away. Had they come after me I'd easily have given them the slip, then gone to check on her."

"Thanks, I appreciate your valor."

"James, what is your request from earlier?" DCS Fordham asked.

"After getting my bags I'd like to see Elizabeth. It won't take but five minutes. It would not be right to leave without telling her goodbye."

"You were correct with your assumption, we can stop by. I'd prefer you not mention Olivia's new role to her."

"I've no intention of telling her. Olivia is good at glossing things over. She can handle that, even though Elizabeth is smarter than Olivia thinks."

"She is definitely a bright girl."

CHAPTER TWENTY

At the Clareridge, I was surprised when Nameless Driver parked and accompanied me to my room. I packed up my old bag plus the new one with the Keswick purchases. It took me five minutes.

"I guess your orders are not to let me out of your sight." I said. "You are preventing a flight risk or dangerous rogue looking to escape. Shoot me in the leg if I go on the lam."

He just looked at me and shrugged.

"That's OK. I wouldn't talk to the mouthy American either."

"A good catch with the stapler note," he finally said. "Someone will be in trouble for missing that."

"But not us, good sir. Or was I supposed to find it?"

He shrugged but said nothing. These spy types were annoying. We walked in silence back to the car. DCS Fordham was on the phone when we arrived but quickly hung up. He seemed pleased to see I had not run off. From there it was only three minutes to Olivia's house. Both of them stayed in the car while I got out to find Elizabeth.

She was in the front garden wearing a flowery dress. Lounging in a chair and reading a book in the sun. She stood and reminded me of a fairy in an English garden, with a clear and innocent face.

"James, I wasn't expecting to see you." She looked past me and saw the car. Then her face changed as she realized Olivia was not with me. "James, where's mum? What has happened?"

"It is OK, Elizabeth. Everything is good and Olivia is fine. The investigation is over and she's been exonerated."

"That is good news. But…"

"What, Elizabeth?"

Her eyes filled with tears and her face contorted into a sob. "I think… I am responsible…"

I took her hands in mine to look her in the face. "No, Elizabeth, you absolutely are not responsible for what happened to Campbell. It's not true because I know what happened."

"What do you mean?"

"I know what happened on the ridge that night. These men in the car saw it happen. When you went back to find Campbell, and he was not there, it was because criminals he was in business with had already killed him. You had nothing to do with it. You are very lucky you were not there at the time or they may have killed you."

"I don't understand."

"I know, but your mum will be home soon and she can tell you more. Just know that nothing happened that is your fault."

"Who are those men?"

"Investigators. They were also working the case but I didn't know it. I'm getting a ride to the airport. Something has come up and I'd best go."

"Is mum really OK?"

"Oh yes, she's fine. I just left her and I've already told her goodbye. She can fill you in on the rest."

"Are you in trouble?"

"Not at all. It is a simple but long story that I don't have time to tell. But I wanted to see you in person before I left."

"You did?"

"Definitely. Although I'm in a hurry I was not going to leave without seeing you."

"Thank you James. For everything. For seeing me before you left."

"You are welcome. Elizabeth, I know a lot has happened. I think, based on my experience, that you should find someone to talk to. A professional that can help you sort out some things."

"I don't think that would be a good idea."

"It is OK. Whatever you discuss there can't ever be released or repeated. Elizabeth, don't let things fester and ruin your life. You have a long and wonderful life left to live. Do it without guilt or regret. Those are things that weigh you down. Just think about it, please."

"I will."

"Sorry, I have to go. I wish I had more time to spend with you. Stay good will you."

"I shall. James, come back to see me."

"I can't come back soon to England because of how the investigation into Campbell has to play out. But I'll figure something out and we can talk."

"Good, I'd like that. Goodbye James."

"Bye Elizabeth."

We hugged for moment. I turned and left her there in the garden. It did not seem right somehow. But life rarely lets us do what we want. I climbed in the car and we drove toward Manchester. These guys were taking exceptional care to see me to the airport.

"Thanks for letting me see her," I said.

"You are welcome," DCS Fordham replied.

"Inspector, I think you played us very well."

"Oh, how is that?"

"You let me run around and stir up things. Then as I got closer to the truth and Olivia was getting more desperate, you stepped in to offer her a way out."

"James, despite what you think of me, wasn't it better to do it this way rather than put Olivia through more of an investigation? I even had a supervisor suggest putting Elizabeth on trial to throw off the Russians to enable us to further investigate them. If not for murder then for assault. I disagreed and thought this a better course of action."

"I think you took my statement wrongly. I was trying to

give you a compliment. I wholeheartedly agree with the outcome."

"Thank you. I'm sorry I didn't give you more time to say goodbye to Olivia."

"No worries, I didn't need to. Elizabeth was the important stop."

"I thought you and Olivia had come to an agreement, grown closer, rekindled the old flame, so to speak."

"Oh no, we did not. We had our time once and never again. I'm not naïve enough to think we would rekindle anything."

"That is unfortunate."

"I don't think so. DCS Fordham, do you know what a rattlesnake is?"

"Not personally. I've seen them on television. Quite poisonous I recall."

"I once bought a property, a larger acreage, to start a farm. Next door was an old abandoned agricultural complex. A group went in to salvage materials from some of the abandoned buildings, mostly old barns. In one day, they killed one hundred and sixty-seven rattlesnakes."

"It must have been unnerving to live beside that."

"No, because I had a few king snakes near the house that chased off and killed the rattlesnakes that approached. I let the kings live in the basement in return for their service."

"I'm not sure how that story fits in to our conversation."

"Sorry, that was background. I have not gotten to the point yet."

"Please continue."

"Rattlesnakes tend to be ill-natured. Once they get

wound up, I've seen them strike repeatedly at anything and everything around them. They can't stop until they get too tired to continue. You don't want to be around that kind of snake. All you can do is kill it."

"That seems prudent."

"But one day I was walking over by that property, where my neighbor's driveway ran through the woods. A nice day and the asphalt was warm. A large rattlesnake, over four feet long was stretched out on the pavement. Nearly as big around as my upper leg. A timber rattler, with a large black velvet patch on the base of the tail, with more than ten rattles. Most likely it was a pregnant female."

"What did you do?"

"I was worried someone would drive over her or stop to shoot her. Both were regular occurrences around there. I found two short sticks that were sturdy. I approached her and worked the sticks under her body, then lifted her up. After walking to the edge of the pavement, I gently laid her in the grass. All the time knowing she had enough venom to kill me ten times over. She chose not too."

"Why did you do that?"

"Because it needed to be done."

"James, you are a strange man. But your story tells me a lot about you. Perhaps also about others I've recently dealt with."

"Perhaps. You will take care of her, won't you?"

"I shall. With two sticks if I have to."

"Thanks. More importantly, please watch over Elizabeth."

"That I will assuredly do."

"Good. I would rather come back to the UK eventually on a positive note instead of coming back to take on the Russian mob."

"We don't want you doing that."

"I also appreciate what you did for Olivia, by omission."

"What do you think I didn't tell her, in order to spare her? That her children were with Campbell on the ridge the night he died? I'm sure I don't know what you're talking about."

"Yeah, that. No reason to burden her. Besides, Elizabeth insisted they left him very much alive. I believe her."

"You should. I have seen the footage."

"The footage of what?"

"A video that doesn't exist. One that shows a night vision image of the two children leaving. Then two men of ill repute and foreign origin arriving and escorting Campbell to the edge of the cliff. You can imagine the rest. Then one of the children coming back, not seeing anything, then leaving again."

"The clumsy fall, Russian style. You had him under surveillance the entire time."

"Surveilled but not protected. His death was a bit premature to our chagrin."

"Then you will do better with Olivia."

"Lesson learned. She'll have a rotating four-person team as I promised. Something else you should not know."

"I know nothing, but again I appreciate it. Still a great plan, knowing about Campbell, but letting Olivia remain a person of interest. Smart."

"A necessary ruse. No longer necessary."

"You have restored my faith in British Intelligence."

"Wish I could return that comment in regard to American Intelligence."

"Yeah, we are a bit off lately."

The conversation tailed off. DCS Fordham went into text mode as I don't think he wanted me to hear his conversations. The Nameless Driver never talked on the ride down.

They dropped me at my terminal. I thought they might go in but didn't. DCS Fordham told me which airline to check in with and they left. I was surprised to find it was a first class ticket like I had flown over with. A gift from the British government. It was probably worth it to them to get rid of me.

After boarding I checked my phone before turning it off. No calls or texts from Olivia. I imagine she was busy getting her new life started. I would have called Elizabeth but decided it was a bad idea. The authorities would frown on it and possibly block me.

I settled in for the long flight. Several hours to contemplate what had just happened. It had ended so abruptly I still did not have my thoughts in order. But I was grateful Olivia was in the clear. Even more so that Elizabeth was not responsible for Campbell's death. Yet I knew she was troubled by her actions on the ridge, regardless of how much Campbell deserved it. I had to trust Olivia would help her find a therapist or someone to assist with her trauma due to Campbell's long term cruelty.

The other thought I kept having was how inconsequential my investigation into Campbell's death had been. I bumbled around not knowing all the deeper moving parts and parties involved before and after his death. That was likely true for any murder, and something I should remember.

The prior cases of murder I had been involved in spoke to the same conclusion. The murderer of the real estate agent was involved in a complex web of illegal activity with real estate deals and various criminal side deals. And the murdered pilot was deep in the layers of the illegal marijuana trade. But worse was his cousin, the killer, also in the business with delusions of grandeur about land full of valuable minerals and elements.

After that I did what I never do. I fell asleep on the plane. My sleep was fitful and filled with odd dreams I didn't remember upon waking.

My first act when getting to my house was spending some time with Kat. She did not sulk, at least not much. We picked up where we left off two weeks ago. I fed her, rubbed her belly, and then we sat outside for a few minutes until she left the porch to go prowl the bushes. That was my cue to go take a walk. I needed to stretch my legs and clear my brain. On the back loop I saw Millard was home and on his porch. I walked up his drive and we traded greetings.

"James, you are looking droopy," Millard said. "Just on the edge of terrible actually. Woman troubles or jet lag?"

"Does it have to be a choice?"

"Oh, that is bad."

"It is not that bad. Just have a lot on my mind and still tired, physically and mentally."

"Anything you want to talk about?"

"Well, give me a moment. I need to think about what is bothering me in order of most to least."

"While you are thinking, did you get the murder and the meth supplier business solved?"

"In a way, yes. The authorities stepped in and everything is resolved."

"Good. Now back to your list. Carry on otherwise I'm not sure I'll live long enough to hear it all."

"OK, I'll summarize before you kick off. I met a woman I used to love and was married to."

"That's bad."

"Actually, not so much. Still didn't get closure but now I realize I don't need it. Nothing really happened but it was a bittersweet experience. Also, I met her daughter who really didn't like me at first. But we got very close although it was only two weeks. I already miss talking to her, and I think she fits into the mold of the daughter I never had."

"That is an interesting quandary. You are sad because your ex-wife's daughter is not yours."

"Not exactly. I mean, I do have that thought, but that is not the source of my unhappiness."

"Then what is?"

"If a person, a powerful person, chooses to do terrible things to the people closest to him, are they, the victims, allowed to end him?"

"James, that is a powerful question. Give me a moment

before I answer. Alright, your answer awaits inside. Follow me."

We went inside to the study on the left. His three rooms full of books were in the back. He rummaged around in a dark wood cabinet. It was full of old bottles of spirits. Soon he found the right one. He took two crystal goblets off a shelf above the cabinet.

"James, I know you don't drink much anymore. Neither do I. But we need to do this before I give you an answer. Consider this a medicinal application."

"Thanks Millard," I said as he handed me the glass with three fingers of amber liquid.

"Follow me." We stepped into one of the three library rooms, the one full of philosophy books. "Now we drink."

It was strong, incredibly smooth, and more buttery than a liquid had a right to be. It was like drinking a pirate ship run aground in a Caribbean butter factory. "Millard, this is wonderful. I have not had anything like this since grad school. A buddy brought a special bottle back from South America."

"It is rum, aged fifty years before bottling. A colleague from long ago gave me this after I did him a favor."

"Must have been quite a favor."

"It was. Now, to get to your question. Take another sip and ask your question out loud."

"Uh, OK. When a powerful man chooses to do terrible things to those closest to him, do they have the right to kill him?" The only answer was silence.

"Do you hear that?"

"No, I don't hear anything."

"That's right."

"This isn't getting me anywhere Millard."

"Oh, but it is. What you have here is more than two thousand volumes, from two thousand men considered the finest thinkers of the human race. Or at least in Western civilization. Nor did the women get published. But anyway, they are all now ghosts. But two thousand ghosts just answered your question. You didn't hear anything because they all shouted at the same time and drowned each other out, resulting in white noise you could not hear. But they gave you two thousand different answers."

"That is quite a story. But I think I have an idea what you're saying."

"Yes, there are two thousand different answers to your question. I know, because I've read every book in here. But what they say does not matter. What I say, after reading all of them, does not matter."

I took another, larger sip. I looked at him to finish.

"All that matters in the end is what you think. You are your own best philosopher. None of those two thousand are you, or know you."

"Thanks Millard. I guess that makes you a philosopher."

"No, I'm too ornery. These people," as he gestured around the room, "bore me to death. I'd rather be a cantankerous old man than a fancy book-writing philosopher."

"I understand that."

"James, don't think less of a good person if they did a bad thing to a bad person. But you already know that."

"I do. But maybe it took two thousand boring ghosts to make me see it."

"See, I told you, those ghosts exist. But if you ever hear them say anything, mind that you do the opposite."

"I will, Millard. Even so, they didn't actually end the bad man, but they wanted to. And probably should have."

"Ah, so is the question really about them, or about yourself? What lengths should you go to in order to end a bad person? I assume someone like the sheriff or Doyle a few months back. Or the murderer that died in your house."

"Yeah, I guess that is what I really want to know."

"Well, those ghosts won't give you a good answer, because once again it is all up to you. When you stand on the precipice, only you can decide whether to step forward or step back."

"Thanks for the drink and the lesson."

"Always happy to help. Have you seen your lady friend since you've been back?"

"No, not yet. I need to call her and ask her over for dinner."

"Best get to it then. Out of my house and off my porch, and get on the phone."

"I will."

Donna had taken me to the airport but I didn't ask her to pick me up. I had a difficult time asking people to intentionally drive to the Atlanta airport. I had taken a car service from the airport back home. But perhaps she would see that as something I did not mean it to be. I wasn't avoiding her. Well, not much.

"Hi Donna."

"Hi James, are you on your way back?"

"I've actually been home a little while. I got a car service home as I didn't want to have you come to Atlanta again."

"It would have been fine, James. It would not have been a problem picking you up."

"I'm glad to hear it, but you know how much I hate that drive. I just assume everyone does. But I wanted to see you and ask if you wanted to come over for dinner?"

"I don't know. Aren't you jet-lagged?"

"No, not coming home. For me, going over is the hard part. Coming back is better, although in a couple days from now I'll probably take an extra long sleep."

"You are so strange. I'm not sure about dinner tonight, but I'd like to come over."

"That's fine. Instead of cooking we can have a drink, take a walk, or just sit on the porch."

"OK, I'll be over in about an hour."

"Sounds great, see you then."

Maybe she wasn't too cross with me. She had been understanding about me going on the trip to help my ex-wife. Something I assumed most women would have been less understanding about. I was optimistic, but still felt a slight unease. I was not sure whether it was due to Donna, Millard's lesson, or something else I had forgotten.

I was sitting on the front porch with Kat when Donna arrived. I had a small pitcher of iced tea mixed with lemonade and two glasses ready. I stood as she parked and came up to give me a quick hug. We sat as I poured us both a drink. No alcohol since it might dull my already diminished senses.

"James, how was your trip? Did you accomplish everything you needed to?"

"It was quite an experience. Seeing places I had not seen in many years. Same with Olivia. In both cases, everything different but somehow fundamentally the same. I guess I did accomplish something by pushing some buttons I should not have. Some special police crawled out of the shadows and let me know I was mucking up their special operation and they tossed me out of the UK."

"That sounds interesting. Was it because of the murder?"

"Yes, some criminals had killed the man, and the police wanted to keep it quiet and run undercover operations. I was glad to have found out though, as I initially suspected the man's stepdaughter, Olivia's child, had killed him."

"That is awful, I'm glad you got that cleared up. But why did you suspect her?"

"The man was a monster and probably deserved it. She and her brother were there with the man, Campbell, the night he was killed. They were there to confront him, and I think possibly do more, but they left instead. Then two Russians came along and tossed him off a cliff before the kids could come back and try it."

"That sounds quite convoluted. But I really wanted to ask how it went with you and your ex."

"Oh, it was quite an adventure. Certainly nothing happened in the way of any romance. That had long been dead and I don't know of anything that could change it. But she was worried her kids were involved in the murder so she tried to keep everything she could hidden from me like we talked about on the phone."

"That sounds like a mom. But not very productive for your investigation."

"No, it was not, but I understood eventually. Something did happen on the trip that was unexpected, however."

"What was it?"

"I seemed to form a close bond with Elizabeth, Olivia's

daughter. She hated me at first, but then we had some frank talks and she changed her mind."

"Maybe she was looking for a decent father figure."

"I think that was exactly what happened. But we also got to the point we could talk to each other. Not as father and daughter, but as two people. I did not expect that with a twenty-year-old, and I don't think she expected that from an old man like me. But I understood her trauma as something similar had happened to Olivia that Elizabeth did not know about. And, of course, Elizabeth and I commiserated over having to deal with Olivia."

"It is nice, James, that you got to have that experience. Will you keep in touch?"

"I'm not sure, but I hope so. Meanwhile she is a young woman in the middle of attending university and experiencing life, so I imagine she will have plenty of other things to do than talk to me."

"You might be surprised. If you impressed her, she might adopt you as a mentor at least."

"Maybe, we will see. How was your last two weeks?"

"It has been good. I've had time to think about things and make some decisions."

"Uh oh."

"What?"

"Nothing, go ahead."

"I'll get right to it. I think we should take a break, and not date or see each other anymore."

"Was there something I did or did not do to spark that?"

"No, I just came to some realizations. Nothing you did."

"OK, I'm not sure what to say next. Just agree with you or try to talk you into not breaking up."

"I think this is for the best, so no reason to talk me out of it. Just agree and I'll go."

"Alright, I'll miss seeing you, but I'll comply with your wishes."

"Thank you for being reasonable. I'm going to go now. I'm glad things worked out overseas and that you made it back. Goodbye James."

"Bye Donna." I stupidly sat on the porch and watched her go. I was being reasonable and calm, but I felt like I had just lost something important. It was so sudden I was not taking in what it really meant. After the emotional tides I'd ridden the past two weeks, this overwhelmed me so I felt numb. I had a feeling this was going to hurt once the numbness wore off. Meanwhile I decided to think about it some other time. Maybe tomorrow, maybe never.

CHAPTER TWENTY-TWO

The next morning I carried on as if everything was normal. I popped Kat into the bike carrier and scooted to the bookstore. I was craving a normal, slow day in Warm Springs. My bookstore, based on the lack of customers, was likely the best place to experience that. I got the slow part right. One customer for the morning and I believe the woman came in to see Kat rather than to buy a book.

Just after noon I put the Closed sign up and stepped over to Mable's. I was not very hungry but I suppose I was looking for human contact. Lottie was not there, at least not up front, which was unusual. I ordered a light lunch as my appetite was running thin. A small omelette with fresh fruit and tea was all I needed. I ate at the counter while the normal world cycled through its regular day.

I left Mable's with a small bag of roast chicken for Kat. She was expecting me as soon as I walked in and snarfed down the first portions, then retired to the window for a full-body lick bath. After a quick nap, she would probably go back and finish the meal. I heard Millard spin into town and park in front of my store. I went to the front door, but he waved as he went into Mable's. Back at my desk I did bookstore stuff. There was little enough going on so I had time to contemplate my recent life and what I planned to do in the future. Warm Springs was a nice and easy place to live, but I wondered about my place in it. Kat must like it just fine as she was napping so hard she was snoring. That should be my new philosophy.

A half hour later, Millard and Lottie came into the store. I decided to go on the offensive since the two of them together must be scheming something. If they got off the first salvo I would never catch up.

"What can I do for you two this fine afternoon? Do you want me to preside over the nuptials? I can get ordained online if you give me five minutes."

"Millard, I told you his condition has deteriorated faster these past few months. By Christmas he'll be picking the raisins out of his oatmeal and trying to grow a vineyard," Lottie said.

"Well Lottie, that is not the dumbest thing I've ever heard. Unless they're seedless raisins," Millard replied.

"Of course all the raisins in oatmeal are seedless, Millard. You are going to be right in that home with him."

"Before you two lovebirds get too excited, why are you here?" I could not remember both of them visiting the store together.

"James, how is business going? Lottie asked.

"Not great. I keep moving along, but it is slow. I'm not gaining much month-over-month so not seeing a good annual growth projection."

"At that rate, how long before you make back your investment?" Millard asked.

I began laughing. "Based on actuarial tables I don't believe my predicted lifespan is long enough to make back the investment."

"That is what we think too." Lottie said. "Have you thought about selling?"

"Not really. It might be something to think about. But despite the lack of profit, I kind of like having a bookstore."

"Of course you do. But is it worth your time and money to keep it?"

"Lottie, you are usually more direct than this. What are you saying?"

"You are right. No more beating those bushes and sending you on a snipe hunt. James, you are not cut out to be a full-time bookstore owner-operator. I know you like it but it's not the best use of your time."

"Harsh, but true enough I guess."

"We have a proposal for you that might solve several different areas," she said.

"OK, go ahead."

"Millard and I want to buy into the bookstore. The three of us would be partners."

"OK, tell me more. What does that look like on a daily basis?"

"I'd be here two days a week, and Millard would take two days. You would still get one or two days depending on the schedule. I'd take on the business end since you've said you didn't like it."

"Are you going to stop working at Mable's?"

"No, I'll do a few shifts. But it is getting too difficult to work six days in a row over there. My days here would be less stressful. I can sit down and use my mind on the business end of things. Handle the taxes, inventory, and ordering. It will be a lot less work than foodservice. This way Millard has a business to attend to and he gets out of the house. But he will be here rather than hanging out with his friends that are a bad influence. What do you think?"

"Haven't seen any financials, but so far it sounds promising. I think you have a deal."

"Good, you can get back to chasing murderers and criminals. I get a break from next door, and Millard has a place to do business. But no card games during open hours, right Millard?"

"Oh, of course not," he said." Strictly books during normal hours. But this is a great site for evening card games."

"Uh, Lottie, maybe some daytime card games could run in the back," I said. "Not high stakes poker, but bridge and pinochle, something like that. Something to get people in the store on a regular basis."

"That might work, James. But Millard, no poker games

with the boys. That's not the business we need. More like Junior League or the Master Gardeners. We need to get Donna back here for another author event. Things like that. What, do you not want to do those anymore?"

"Just schedule Donna for a day when I won't be here."

"James, what did you do?" Lottie asked.

"Nothing in particular, or at least she did not tell me. Just the old line that it was her, not me, and some yada yada. So she does not want to continue seeing me."

Instead of going after me, which I expected, Lottie moved over to sit beside me. "I'm sorry, James. I hope you two can work it out, or if not you can get on with your life."

"Thanks Lottie. That is my plan."

"Getting you out of this lonely store is even a better idea, then. I'll have papers for us to review soon. Do you have a lawyer?"

"Not exactly. But I have an ex-lawyer that can help me with this."

"Who?"

"Lawrence K Endicott, the fourth." Larry was a lawyer I had framed, who then flipped and gave up many of the criminals in the region for whom he had formed shell companies and other entities.

Lottie and Millard began laughing. "How in the world did that happen?" Lottie asked.

"He's still going to his office over in Hamilton. I stopped by to talk to him. Since then we've been working on some ideas."

"Did you tell him yet that you were the one that got him in trouble?" Millard asked.

"I did. He wasn't happy, but he said that getting arrested and disbarred was the best thing that has happened to him. It got him out of working for all the crooks in the region. He got into it almost by accident, then became used to the easy money. However, he was in so deep that he felt he was months away from being killed. He was nervous all the time, and it was so bad he did not know which of a half dozen criminals would kill him first to protect their secrets and assets. I told him because if you are going to ruin someone's life, even for a good cause, you should own up to it and accept the consequences."

"Well, let him know we will have some partnership papers to review."

"I will. And thanks Lottie and Millard. I believe I need a change and getting away from the store on a daily basis is a good start."

They left and I had time to think about what was happening and what it meant for me. Instead of being sad about losing most of the business I had started, I felt like a weight was being lifted. I could have the best of both worlds. I still had a share of the bookstore and could work there occasionally, but I would no longer be 100% responsible for it, either financially or by attendance. The town would continue to have a bookstore and, depending on what Millard and Lottie did, possibly even something of a community center. It somehow felt right. Although early, I gathered up Kat, put up the Closed sign, and pedaled home.

I called Larry and let him know I'd be coming to see him with papers. I wondered once again if I had done the right thing by telling him I was the one that framed him. It seemed the honorable thing to do. But if he was still talking to any of the criminals he ratted out and they knew my role, they might not be happy with me. But that was a long list, so a few more did not matter.

Before I did anything else I sat on the porch and watched Kat make her rounds in the yard. I knew better to make anymore major decisions in my life. The UK trip had left me a little discombobulated, then Donna dumping me was a letdown.

But the bookstore offer was a nice surprise. Being unsuccessful was not a great feeling, but I knew it was a risk. Cutting my losses seemed the right thing to do.

A day later I had the partnership papers. Lottie had obviously already had them in progress before talking to me. As usual she was way ahead of me. I drove to Hamilton to see my disbarred legal advisor.

"Larry, here are the papers I mentioned. Two people want to buy into the bookstore and share equal partnership with me."

"I'll take a look and let you know. You are already aware of some of the pitfalls of partnerships I presume?"

"Some, yes. I'm hoping after you review the papers you can tell me all the many ways it can go bad."

"I will. But tell me, is it something you want to do?"

"I think so."

"Then no reason to tell you the bad stuff. You will do it anyway."

"Probably. I also have another question for you, on a totally different topic."

"Is it going to get me into trouble? You have a knack for that."

"I don't think so, but once again I have to rely on your experience. As always, if it puts you in jeopardy then don't do it. But during your previous iteration as a lawyer doing dirty deals, I ran across some papers where you did business with Benjamin Rawley."

"I remember him. A pompous bureaucrat from the Warm Springs campus. His only positive characteristic is that he knows a few powerful people at the Statehouse in Atlanta. He and some others were planning to run a series of illegal operations culminating in a condominium development on the Warm Springs campus. I remember it stopped abruptly after you killed the principal architect of the scheme."

"First of all, Joe was not a principal architect, merely a greedy real estate agent. Maybe a mid-level worker bee. Second of all, I was responsible for his death but I did not kill him."

"Speaking as a former lawyer, what's the difference?"

"Uh, none really. Anyhow, I assume the vast information you turned over to the authorities was only part of your vast files and knowledge of the multiple criminal enterprises. Surely you kept some to protect yourself in case they had plans to come after you."

"I could not say for sure without incriminating myself."

"Well said. But if by divine intervention a file on Benjamin dropped from the sky I would appreciate being somewhere near the drop zone."

"I can arrange those logistics. But divinity won't be a part of it. Theoretically speaking, do you want the kind of information that can blackmail him, get him fired, or get him killed?"

"That is a conundrum. All three? Just kidding, I think getting him fired and out of his position to cause mischief is good enough. Although I once thought I had enough evidence of his wrongdoing to make that happen. But somehow he survived."

"He won't survive what is coming. You sure you don't want to squeeze him first? I think you might be surprised what he is involved with."

"Tempting, but no. Unless it is something that might be bad for the campus."

"I'll think about it and forward to you if it is."

"I do appreciate it. Same fee as usual?"

"You bet. I'll put it on your tab."

CHAPTER TWENTY-THREE

During renovations of the small guest cottage behind my house, I had found a glass bottle containing a letter. It was faded so I had it scanned and analyzed at the University of Georgia. The result was somewhat shocking, as it detailed a double murder in Warm Springs back in the early 1940s. A local boy that worked at the Warm Springs Institute was murdered by the jealous male fiancé of a patient. The boy's murder was immediately avenged; the female fiancé killed her betrothed for killing the boy. Then both murders were covered up, one by staging it as a train accident and the other by burying the body and disappearing it forever.

One portion of the letter that was the least legible, possibly because it was the outer page, needed some extra analysis. It described something other than those two murders, introducing the possibly related murder of a third person. I had decided to research available archives and look for proof of the first two murders on my own. I did so because the buried body was likely located on or near the golf course, possibly even under our community garden. If true, I needed to handle it carefully as it could cause repercussions on campus. It might even cause the closure of the garden.

The potential third murder was much more public and occurred far away from campus. But because it might be related, and included a Warm Springs Institute former employee, I decided to farm out that story to a third party for investigation. The victim was purported to be an important intelligence asset so Millard's Octoposse seemed the best option to ferret out the truth. Thus the package I left for him before I went to Britain. I expected he would have his people working on it and he would have been giving me updates. But so far he had said nothing. Maybe he had not made any progress, but I knew he kept up with campus history more than anyone. If anyone knew about the person and their murder it would be Millard.

The excerpt was compelling if true. President Roosevelt's tranquil retreat might have been much more complex than I imagined. But it made sense since a lot of decisions affecting the world during the 1930s and 1940s were made in Warm Springs. I reread the excerpt.

· · ·

I READ *the headline one morning and it frightened me something awful. Verona White, WAC Private, formerly of Manchester and an employee of the Roosevelt Warm Springs Institute, was murdered in Ohio.*

I am writing this account after learning of Verona's murder and a series of other events. I had known Verona for years. She was who helped move and bury the body of that awful boy. Whether or not her murder is related I don't know, but if the Griswold family suspected we were involved in his murder, they have the resources to take such action.

Accounts report a mysterious "woman in black" and an unidentified man in the hotel and elevator at the time of Verona's killing. I saw such a woman matching the description walking through the campus. A man I did not know accompanied her. This happened one week before the report of Verona's death. Then yesterday I saw the woman again. Although it has been two years, I am sure it was her. That has prompted me to record the events as best as I recall. If I am next then if nothing else this text shall remain to tell the tale.

I did not know her well at first. Verona spent most of her time when she was on campus working with the naval personnel. There was a rumor she was more than an Institute employee. I heard the Navy had recruited her to covertly investigate the America First movement, the group headed by Lindbergh that favored Nazi Germany and strove to keep America out of the war. I did not then, nor to this day, know if that was true. But if I heard the rumor, then I wonder about who else might have heard it. Nazi intelligence operatives were active in America in 1943.

Whether the Nazi's or the Griswold family were involved,

Verona was murdered under mysterious circumstances. I am concerned about the other deaths with which I was involved. They were murders as well, and I feel terribly guilty about the part I played.

BECAUSE MILLARD HAD YET to mention the letter and material I had left with him, I went to his house to ask about it. Something unusual was going on. As I walked the outer loop I saw his vehicle and knew he was home. Walking up he came out the front door with a pitcher and two glasses. He was wearing a vest with vertical stripes of alternating blue and yellow. I still had not caught him with the same vest on twice.

"Come on up on the porch," he said. "I've been expecting you."

"What's in the pitcher?"

"Truth serum. Lemonade base with cranberry juice and a couple of shots of vodka."

"That should help the truth along."

"We'll see. Now what did you come here after?"

I told him what I knew about finding the letter and the portion of the letter detailing the first two murders. That was the lead-in to the portion I had given him, since they might be related. I also told him my minimal research had uncovered on the murderer of the local boy. His family, the Griswold's, were rabid America First members. A large number of wealthy Americans, fronted by Charles Lindbergh, believed America should not get into a war in Europe. That was a kind way of saying those people were German sympathizers, or more appropriately, Nazi sympathizers. Some were outright bribed by the Nazis, and others fully supported the Nazi policies. Because of their wealth and position they had an outsized influence on American politics at the time. The only thing they were more passionate about than support for the Germans was their hatred of Franklin D. Roosevelt. They felt FDR was guilty of treason for the Lend-Lease program worked out with Churchill to get England more ships and war material.

Millard sat quietly and with no expression. I realized he already knew everything about what I said. I tried a new question.

"Do you know who the author of the letter was?" I asked.

"I do not. But I would very much like to know."

"Millard, you have been unusually quiet about the letter. What is going on?"

"I was not sure I would ever talk to you or anyone about this. But things have lain secret and dormant long enough. Have I ever told you about my father?"

"No, not really."

"He was what once was called a Renaissance man. A term I don't like because it suggests there are no Renaissance women, which is absurd, there have been plenty. Anyway, he was an excellent musician, decent singer, good writer, spoke six languages, and physically fit. Plus many other attributes that would normally propel someone of his talents into fame and fortune. Yet almost no one has ever heard of him."

"I'm sensing a story. Why was he not famous?"

"He gave his loyalty to his country and to the man

representing it. Now before I tell you the rest of his story, I have to tell you about the setting. Which was here in Warm Springs, on this campus. I think few people realize how important this place was for a few years. Important enough that there was international intrigue and influence happening constantly. FDR's frequent presence here while president brought all that attention. It had to be dealt with in a quiet and expeditious manner. That was what my father did. Quietly enough he was never noticed and that was why no one ever knew about his skills."

"He was a fixer for FDR?"

"He was, but also a fixer for anything that happened in FDR's orbit anywhere he went, except in Washington, DC. There were others assigned just to DC. But anytime FDR left DC my father was close by, yet never seen or heard. Because of that role, I may have some knowledge of what was recorded in that letter."

"I'd like to hear it."

"I'll start somewhat backwards, and will probably circle around more than once. But I will finally get to the point."

I poured a glass of serum and prepared for what I believed would be a long story. Millard poured himself a drink.

"Verona was from Warm Springs, although she told everyone she was from Manchester. A tiny ruse, one of many. She worked here at the Institute and was recruited to keep an eye on the America First group. Because there were some wealthy patients and families on campus that adhered to that nonsense. Soon enough, her role expanded.

"The Nazis had spent a lot of time, money, and effort recruiting wealthy and influential Americans. Knowing that, counterintelligence suggested using that same network against the Nazis. Operation Nightshade was begun in 1936 to feed influence back to the Nazis. Much more subtle than feeding them simple misinformation, it pushed ideas back to the Nazis that ultimately were not in their best interest. One of the main goals was to get Germany to turn on its allies. The first target was Italy, but that did not work as planned. Although Hitler did come to distrust Mussolini. One of the real successes of the effort was convincing those around Hitler to exert their influence and attack Russia. Had that not happened, Europe would now be speaking German, or Russian in the eastern countries.

"Verona seemed a likely candidate to be part of the misinformation and influence machine aimed at the Nazis. She got married and moved north with her husband. Up there, she went to what amounted to espionage school. Then she and her husband publicly separated. Honestly, I'm not sure they were ever married or whether it was a front. I suspect he was also in the program. Anyway, she ended up joining the WACS, or Women's Army Corps and went to Ohio. There were strong rumors that not only America First, or AF sympathizers were joining the service, but also a few actual Nazis. Her job was to find them."

"Was she supposed to eliminate them?"

"No, first to identify and then cultivate them. Give them ideas to pass back to the German regime. She put on a fierce free partying persona, juggling multiple boyfriends and hosting wild weekends."

"I guess it's easier to influence a young man with booze

and sex, which probably has been happening for ten thousand years."

"It is not only easy, it is effective. Then she was found dead in what was an obvious staged event, made to look like a jealous boyfriend killed her."

"Millard, how do you know all this? I assume your father did not tell you when you were young."

"No, he didn't, at least not in the way you might think. Let's go to the basement. I need your help with something."

"OK."

CHAPTER TWENTY-FOUR

Down the steps, he turned on a light. The entire basement lit up. I was expecting a dark, dank space with cobwebs. Instead it was a painted white floor, with row upon row of glass and wood display cases filled with rocks and minerals. He had mentioned he collected rocks and kept them in the basement, but this was surreal. I'd seen worse collections in museums. But that was not what he wanted me to see.

"Here, on this foundation wall, is a false block of granite," Millard said. "I need you to work it out of the wall. Try this flat bar. Once you get it worked out an inch or so it will be easy to pull out with your fingers, since it's only two inches deep."

I did as he suggested and used the flat bar in the joint to work out the block, then pull it free. It was not a full block, just a thin granite facade made to look like one of the foundation blocks. Without knowing it was there it would be nearly impossible to spot. In the space behind the facade was a metal door. Millard handed me a key. Using my phone as a flashlight, I could see a lock in the metal and inserted the key. I turned it and the metal door opened.

"Now reach in and grab the metal box within and pull straight out."

I did and was surprised to find the box was approximately eight inches wide and four inches tall, but two feet long. It made a strange sound as I pulled it out.

"The cavity is lined with glass. Keeps the moisture out but screeches something terrible. Should have been lined with lead."

"Why lead?"

"I've told you a little about my father, but not nearly everything. He took long trips out west when I was small, then started going to Augusta, Georgia. Later, he was diagnosed with a very unusual cancer, which was what killed him. Truman did not want my father and his colleagues anywhere around him after Roosevelt died. But they were too valuable to discard. They were dispersed to other highly secret projects but kept away from the new president."

"Why didn't Truman want them around?"

'Some of it was the distaste about what my father and others did to keep Roosevelt safe. Mostly it was his disagreement of the way Roosevelt conducted business. You know much about management styles?"

"Too much, actually."

"Well, Roosevelt's was not a particularly good one, although at times it was effective. He believed in keeping people compartmentalized, then pitting them against each other. He believed the competition would eventually bring forth the best answer."

"Yet we know that system is deeply flawed and detrimental to those forced to participate. It becomes only about winning, and the snakes get to the top, not the best ideas or people. Yeah, I bet Truman did want to get away from that."

"Based on his trips and cancer, you might guess which program my father ended up with."

"Nuclear power, or more precisely nuclear weapons."

"Yes, and it killed him. When I went looking for what I suspected was down here, I used a Geiger counter. I had originally used it when my father became ill. Running it over his body, I found he was radioactive, as I suspected. I believed his journals would be as well, since he was writing a lot in his final months.

"A few times I had found him in the basement near this spot. More than once, he acted as if he'd been caught doing something. I've told you I was once a geologist and collected rock and mineral samples around the world. During that time I took a Geiger counter with me. Both to help find certain deposits but also to know which samples not to collect and bring home. I didn't want to bring back a highly radioactive sample in my pocket and leave it in my house. It did not take me long to find the hiding spot."

"What else was or is in this box?"

"A lot of secrets you don't want to know, and a lot of things that explain what happened and why back in the day. Things he should not have recorded but did."

"Is there anything specific in there to Verona's murder?"

"No, but there is some conjecture over who did it and why. He wanted to pursue it but was assigned other more important tasks for Roosevelt. After Roosevelt died, my father was reassigned and did not get to follow the cold leads, although he wanted to."

"The letter you found adds a new element to Verona's murder. There were a lot of theories about who killed her and why, from a jealous boyfriend to a serial killer. The few of us that knew her role as an undercover operative assumed it was AF or a Nazi cell. Now it could be the family of the young man that was killed by his young lady fiancé. Although the family was AF the motivation may have been their son's murder if they discovered Verona's part in it. Either way, they had motivation and the means to conduct it."

"Where do I go from here?"

"Probably to the deep archives, the ones near Atlanta and the other one in New York. You might find what you are looking for since everyone else alive at the time are now dead."

"What are you going to do with your father's records?"

"That, James, is a conversation for another day."

I put the box back and left Millard's house, knowing more than when I went but still full of questions. My next task was on the way home. Well, not exactly but still on campus.

I knew from the letter the Griswold body was buried along the golf course. The author of the letter knew the head greenskeeper and he was in the process of repairing a water main break and adding another line. The work was done and the crew had nothing left to do but fill in the sizable hole, so the author knew they could bury the body there just deep enough that the crew would never suspect when they covered the rest of it. It would be gone and forgotten.

I had looked up a few old schematics and drawings for the golf course and surroundings the maintenance department kept. Ernie was happy to let me look at them since almost no one else ever visited them and asked questions. I needed to know if the existing road was in the same place as it was in the 1940s. At the time it was likely a single-lane dirt road, and now it's a double-lane paved road. I had to adjust my measurements.

The author had also recorded the distance from the road to the body in paces. My pace length was likely different from theirs, so the map of waterlines was crucial. The road ran along the golf course for nearly 2000 feet, and our garden was along the route. I hoped our little plot was not sitting on a grave and the odds were strongly against it. Once I found where the old water main was and a T-line was added I should be able to pinpoint the body location.

I had just finished my measurements when I saw Bryan. He was driving on his round of campus and happened by. I needed to talk to him anyway.

"How is it going these days?" I asked Bryan.

"Quiet, which is exactly how I like it. Two murders on my watch are two more than I ever wanted."

"Yeah, I agree. But to add to that last one, I found out something else. Not sure what it means but figured you would want to know."

"Great, just what I needed. Did you find another body?" Huh, he had no idea.

"Sort of, but alive. That video from the Fish and Game Department, where we saw Doyle's truck? I sent it to a buddy of mine at UGA. Al looked at it and ran it through some fancy evaluations."

"I don't think I like where this is going."

"Al could not confirm Doyle was the driver using all his tricks, but he said it was about an 80% chance it was Doyle based on facial recognition."

"Oh, OK, that is alright. I'm happy with 80% considering all the other evidence we have, especially the positive DNA test proving Mike Vickers was in the truck."

"Yeah, but that wasn't the important part. Somebody was in the passenger seat."

"That is bad, James. That means I've got a co-conspirator or accomplice, and possible murderer still running around."

"The good news is he's only about 90% sure there was another person. So there is a slight chance there is not another person."

"I don't suppose he could identify the passenger?"

"Not at all. But I wanted to tell you so you can forward the clip to whoever at the state might be able to decipher it."

"I will do that. But I'm not confident we have the best

people. You know they are going to ask me how I know about the second person."

"Go ahead and tell them it was me. They already hate me. If they want Al's contact at UGA I can give it to them."

"Thanks, James. You know how to make my life interesting."

"Just spreading the interesting around."

"I'm leaving before your toss any more grenades in my direction."

"Well, now that you mention it…"

"What? I knew I should have already left."

"Those two septic tanks you dug up on the sheriff's property Did it look like they had been buried for a while?"

"Yes, I would say they had been there for some time. That is why they were difficult to find."

"If you remember, I saw three new ones on the trailer. I found one, but there might be two other new ones somewhere else."

"Yes, I should have left by now. You just gave me a new headache to worry about."

"No, I did not. I actually gave you two new headaches to worry about. So what are you doing out here?"

"Bryan, you really don't want to know. If I told you would have three new big headaches instead of two."

"Is it going to result in imminent danger to anyone?"

"Not at all.

"Then I don't need to know until you tell me."

"That is an admirable philosophy."

"Thanks, James. Goodnight."

"Good evening, Bryan."

He gave me a desultory wave and pulled off. I had sent

Al the video a few months ago. It was a while before he got around to the analysis, again using one of his students during an idle time between research projects. He called three days ago with the news. I was going to tell Bryan immediately but a day or two likely would not matter months after the murder. I had hoped the passenger was the sheriff, but the data was too sparse to give any identification. Maybe Bryan would get lucky with the Georgia Bureau of Investigation and nail the sheriff with a murder charge. Otherwise he was due out in twenty years. I wanted him incarcerated a lot longer than that.

I went home knowing the worst. Based on the best measurements I could make, the letter writer and Verona had buried the body on the edge of the golf course. Almost assuredly under the campus community garden.

CHAPTER TWENTY-FIVE

Standing in front of my house, I'd just gotten out of my car, the one I called the tank, after a grocery run. I took a step toward the house and started to reach down for Kat when things went badly astray. Immediately behind my head a part of the metal and plastic rack on top of the tank exploded and instantly I felt as if a wasp had stung me on back of my neck. Pure instinct took over as I'd had enough bee and wasp stings in my life that I jumped three feet to the side and ducked while dropping my bag of groceries. The move rarely worked with determined yellowjackets or hornets but it made me think I was evading the next sting. Kat had immediately taken off for the backyard.

As the seconds of time passed I realized two important but discordant pieces of information. My rack had exploded for no good reason, and I'd heard a sound from across the field that sounded familiar. But it could not have been a gunshot since hunting was not allowed on campus.

Thinking that thought, I wisely dropped to the ground. Had I heard more than one shot? I really could not remember. The pain in my neck was intense and I reached up to find it freely bleeding. It dawned on me that some idiot was poaching deer and had nearly killed me. I heard someone jogging across the gravel lot next door, the police department house.

"Bryan?" I yelled.

"Yeah, James, what is happening?"

"Stop! Do not come around those bushes. Someone nearly shot me and they might still be out there across the field. Must be a poacher."

"OK, I'm calling this in. Silly since the office is just a few feet away. But Edna can relay it to everyone. Are you hurt?"

"Yes, I caught some shrapnel from where a bullet hit the car."

"Do you need an ambulance?"

"I don't think so, but I can't tell for sure. All I know is the back of my neck is bleeding."

"You are getting an ambulance whether you want one or not." I heard him calling in the shots fired and one person down into his radio. Seconds later I heard the first siren. That should scare off the moron in the woods.

Crouched low, Bryan came around the bushes and vines separating my house from his department building, really just another house on campus. Smartly he stayed behind my car, then scooted over to where I was lying on the edge of my flower bed.

"Have you seen or noticed anything else?" he asked.

"No, nothing."

"Let me look at your neck. OK, a lot of blood coming from an ugly gash. Neck and head wounds, even small ones, bleed a lot. But looks shallow although there could be something buried in there. From the look of your SUV rack there was lots of stuff flying around."

A police car with lights and sirens pulled into my drive. Bryan was telling them on the radio to drive over to the next road and scout the field as soon as backup arrived. Thirty seconds later an ambulance pulled in. One of the perks of living less than a mile from the hospital. A second police car pulled up and then both of them left to drive the hundred yards to the woods on the other side of the field. Bryan had been feeding them specific directions on the radio.

Two young men from the ambulance ran to me with bulky bags. One was talking to Bryan while the other was asking me my name and other information. At the same time he was examining my neck. Standard practice to determine whether I was coherent or in shock. I calmly answered him and assured him I was not going into shock, and really wanted to check on my cat. If he could give me some Novocaine and a bandaid, I'd be happy to quit bothering them. He looked at me like I was crazy, and I realized it might not have been the right thing to say at the moment.

The other one began unpacking the bag, making me think they were going to roll me up like a mummy and roll me into the ambulance. The first one told me they were giving me an IV and taking me to the hospital as it seemed there was debris in my neck wound. I told him thanks and in that case I understood. No reason to get an infection as I had not washed my car lately. Again he looked at me like I was incoherent. Bryan was smiling and told him I was acting normal, because I was always strange. Now he was looking at Bryan like he was incoherent. Bryan had to assure him everything was normal. It was our way of communicating. The guy shook his head and continued on with his EMT business, which was applying a bandage on my neck, an IV in the arm, and some kind of monitor stuck to my chest. The two deputies checking on the woods gave Bryan an all clear, so a minute later I was in the ambulance for a two-minute ride to the hospital.

Since I was an emergency and one of the few patients in the hospital at the moment, I was quickly put in a room off the ER after a two-minute admittance. All they needed was my insurance card apparently. Then I was sent to get scanned and quickly afterward a doctor showed up. She appeared to be about forty, attractive but professional. I really liked her shoes, the same brand I wore. She was probably working off a med school loan by working in a rural area.

"Mr. Wilder?"

"No."

"Your chart shows you as Mr. James Wilder."

"You can call me James, or Dr. Wilder, but Mr. Wilder was my dad and he's dead. I'm not there yet."

"Are you sure?"

"If not this is a weird version of heaven, or maybe purgatory."

"Your goals seems to be higher than your current circumstances warrant."

"Oh, sorry. Then you must be Dr. Satan."

"Not quite there yet. But you will think that after I clean that gash on your neck. You've got a few bits of material in there that must come out."

"Just leave them in so I can set off the metal detectors."

"I am tempted to do that. But my profession requires I remove them to prevent infection."

"Then let's go with your professional standards."

"I'll need to numb the area first. Otherwise this will be unpleasant." She injected a local sedative that stung some.

"Are you going to stick with Doc Satan or do you have a real name?"

"Doctor Hoffman at your service."

"Did you get stuck here working off a loan?"

"Sort of. But I chose this assignment. I've always liked history, and for a rural site this place has lots of it."

"Sure does. I live on campus, where I got shot. I'm still researching the history of the place."

"I assume an errant hunter or a kid target practicing got a shot close enough to nick your neck."

"Nope. Contract hit."

She laughed. "OK, don't tell me."

"Really. That is why there is a police officer just outside."

She stopped getting her tray of instruments and supplies ready. She glanced out of the room then took another look at me.

"Don't worry, I'm not dangerous or a criminal. But I made someone mad."

She smiled. "I can easily understand you did. But most people don't get shot because of it."

"I'm lucky that way."

"Wait, are you the James Wilder that poisoned a killer?"

"Uh, well, sort of. At least the same guy, but the poisoning was just luck on my part. He died before he killed me."

"Then you get nearly killed a lot."

"A lot more than I'd like."

"OK, I'm going to begin. You can keep talking if you like. It won't affect the cleaning and may take your mind off what I'm doing."

"So you have heard about me?"

"Just that a local writer and bookstore owner was checking into a murder, then poisoned the murderer."

"I guess that is accurate. But he drank the poisoned whisky on his own. Although I did not warn him beforehand it was deadly. Probably because he had a gun pointed at me and was about to shoot me in the head."

"That is quite a story."

"Ouch."

"Sorry, that piece was the deepest one. I'll be done in another minute. Seems like you got lucky again."

"I suppose so. Hope I have seven lives left."

"Are you part cat?"

"Just the part that tends to my cat. Or rather, me the servant that cares for her highness."

"I have a cat at home too. Keeps me company and does not seem to mind my strange hours."

"Probably plotting to learn how to drive and work the ATM. After that you will be in the hospital."

"You could be right. I'm putting a bandage over the wound but not stitching you up. I want it to drain and make sure the antibiotic is effective. I'll check you in the morning to make sure everything looks good."

"You are going to have to tie me down to keep me in here overnight."

"We can do that. Put sedative in your IV and cuff you while you are asleep. But that should not be necessary. We need to make sure no infection pops up in that neck wound or you could be in serious trouble."

"OK, that makes sense. I'm all yours for the evening."

"You go from difficult to docile. Should we test you for schizophrenia while we have you?"

"Nah, I can ace that test. Or maybe I can't. We will never know, will we? Schrodinger's psych test."

"OK, so some other form of insanity. Or is that just your strange sense of humor?"

"Your diagnosis appears solid, doctor. Do I have you all shift?"

"Unfortunately, yes. So I'll go ahead and prescribe the sedative so I won't have to deal with you."

"Eminently sensible, doc."

"Get some rest, Dr. Wilder. I'll be by in a few hours."

"Enjoy your evening and go kill some pathogens." She didn't bother to answer. Professional banter was dead.

Bryan came in before they transferred me to a regular room.

"James, I don't think that was a poacher," he said. "I believe you were the target. My guys found nothing to indicate it was a hunter. I went over the area myself and saw little, other than one bush that had been trimmed. I think that is where the shots came from."

"That makes sense. I noticed the policeman outside my room. I guess somebody took the contract."

"What?"

"I had word a while back that someone might take out a contract to kill me."

"You didn't think to tell me about this?"

"I forgot about it."

"Seriously, maybe those EMTs were right. I think there is something wrong with you. Did you hear about a contract from your Atlanta people?"

"Yes, but they didn't think it would happen. If it was in play, then they would warn me to give me time to leave or get prepared."

"I assume you did not get a warning."

"No, I didn't. But it is likely the contract went to somewhere else, or somebody decided to save the money and do it themselves."

"Any idea who was behind the contract?"

"No, I don't know, and neither did the people in Atlanta. Other than it was a long list of local suspects as I have made a lot of people mad around here."

"That you have. I'm not happy it might be someone local however. Do you think it was someone associated with Doyle or the sheriff?"

"Could be either one. Plus they told me the crooks looking to profit from the real estate scams on campus and on Pine Mountain could be involved."

"That does not narrow it down much. Maybe half the people in Hamilton County could want you dead."

"Probably more like 40%. It will take me a little longer to reach a plurality of hatred."

"At least you have goals."

"You said shots, as in plural. I only noticed one."

"Definitely two. One smashed your roof rack on the Landcruiser. The second was just over a little to the side and we found where it hit a tree."

"I guess I was too busy reacting to notice the second shot. Was it just over to the side where I was lying on the ground?"

"Yes, on that side, about head high."

"They missed my head twice. Should have gone for the center mass shot."

"You are lucky he did not."

"My luck is going to run out one day."

"Exactly what I was thinking. I'll come pick you up tomorrow when they release you. We have some investigating to do. Don't go trying to sweet talk Dr. Hoffman into releasing you early. Although after talking to you she might want you gone."

"Hey, you must have overheard our conversation."

"No, but I figured you had already worked your reverse charm and irritated her. Which is good since you already have a girlfriend."

"You are right on the first one, wrong on the second."

"Say that again?"

"I have already irritated Hoffman, and I don't have a girlfriend. Donna wanted to take a break."

"Oh. What kind of break?"

"The only kind that matters. The 'it is not you, it is me' kind of break. The one that does not get unbroken."

"Are you sure?"

"Yeah, I'm pretty sure. Why?"

"I see her coming down the hall."

"That should not be happening."

"Should or not, it is happening. I'll leave you two alone." Bryan winked at me and was gone. I heard him and Donna exchange hellos. Then they had a brief conversation that I could not hear. Another minute and she came in.

"James, are you OK?" she asked.

"Very much, other than a cut on the neck from a piece of roof rack."

"Really, I can't leave you alone for an afternoon without you getting shot."

"Actually you were leaving me alone for a much longer time than that, according to our previous conversation."

"James, just because we are not dating doesn't mean we are not friends or that I don't care about you. Not seeing you was something I meant only in a romantic way. Don't go sulking and acting as if I've harmed you. We are too old for that."

"You are right. But we are also too old for that line you used about it being about you, not me. A typical phrase when a woman doesn't tell a man why she really decided to end things. If you can be honest with me, then we will be friends."

"That is awfully direct. But I agree. I should have told you what I really thought."

"Please do. I won't go trying to change your mind or giving excuses."

"I just don't think we were going anywhere. A lot of wheel spinning with no direction. I know at first we talked about just being with someone and enjoying life. But lately I've been thinking about something more serious. I want to get married again, I think. I don't know why my attitude changed, it just did. And I don't think you are ready for that."

I took a minute to respond as I needed to think about what she was saying and how I really felt. I had to be as honest with her as she was with me. Instinctively, I knew she was right if she now was looking to get married. No matter how I felt about her, the idea of having her or anyone in my presence full-time, with either her living in my house or me living in hers, was not what I wanted to do right now. And I could not be unfair to her and tell her to wait for me.

"Thank you for being honest. I agree with what you are saying. I care for you, a lot. I could even see us getting married. But not right now. I don't know why I feel that way, I just don't want to get married again right now."

"I know, and that is why I needed to stop and decide what to do. Are we still friends?"

"Absolutely. But I probably won't come to your wedding. Unless I know the guy."

"What do you mean?"

"Donna, you are a very desirable woman for many reasons. If you want to get married, I bet you'll be engaged in six months with all the guys out there dying to be with you."

"Thanks for the compliment, I think."

"You are welcome. A year or more from now, when I'm ready to think about marriage, you'll be gone. And I would never ask you to wait, because that would be wrong for both of us."

"Thank you, James, for understanding. Now who is trying to shoot you?"

"The list is too long right now to even guess. Could be one of your wannabe suitors, trying to get me out of the way."

"I doubt that. Now stop joking. This is serious as you nearly got killed."

"I know. But I won't be able to do much sleuthing until I get out of here tomorrow. I'll start systematically going through all the usual suspects and checking the list for new ones."

"Do you think it might be Jeffers or one of his men?"

"The former sheriff is in the top twenty suspects. I'll have to look at him, or rather if he had someone do it. But the list is quite long. You did not know it, but not dating me might have prolonged your life."

"You are not getting rid of me that easily. I'm going to hang around and help you solve this."

"OK, but you've been warned. Now since you are here, can you hand me that cup of ice?"

After Donna left, I was so bored I began thinking. I decided I needed to investigate this as if I was the dead body, because I almost was. I needed a motive, weapon, and a short list of suspects. If I cleared all of them, I would go on to another list. What I did not know was whether a local person took the shots at me or if it was hired out. If hired, I'd likely need the assistance of my people in Atlanta, the Dixie Mafia. Although I did not want to, contacting them first might be smart. They could help me rule out a contract hitter, leaving me with the local population. Only a few dozen were on that list, and most of them were unknown to me. Should be easy.

EPILOGUE

My phone rang and I saw the +44 country code. This should be interesting, if I decided to answer it. Was it Olivia or the DCS Fordham?

"Hello."

"James?" I was too surprised to respond for a second once I heard her voice. "Are you there?"

"Elizabeth, sorry, I was surprised to hear from you. I saw the country code and assumed it was someone else."

"I can guess who. Is this a bad time for you to talk?"

"Absolutely not. It is great to hear from you. I wanted to call but wasn't sure if it was a good idea. Nor did I know if you'd be able to call."

"I think I can, or at least they haven't forbade it. Mum told me a bit about what is happening."

"Then you know there might be others on this line besides us."

"I know, but I wanted to talk to you anyway."

"Sure, what's up?"

"I have been talking to someone, a therapist, at uni. I think it is helping."

"That is great."

"It is. I also wanted to ask, is it OK if I call you sometimes?"

"It is, Elizabeth. I'll look forward to it. Anytime you want please call me."

"I shall. The therapist suggested it would help to speak to…"

"Someone besides your family that you can trust."

"Yes."

"You know, sometime if you travel to America let me know and we can meet. I won't be going to the UK in the near future."

"Thank you, I'd like that. I am on the list to spend summer studying in Amsterdam. Not sure if it will happen this summer or next."

"I might have to come visit you. Its one of my favorite cities. Enough to have lived there for a time."

"That would be fun. James?"

"Yes?"

"Sometimes, lately, I have this scene going through my mind. Like a daydream but more lucid and vivid. In it, I see my mum and an American meeting and falling in love. They get married and have kids, Ian and me. We grow up in a wonderful house. We are all happy."

"Elizabeth, I have had the same scene in my head."

"Really?"

"Yes. But to be honest, I usually have to switch your mom out to someone else."

Elizabeth burst out laughing. "Oh, oh, that is funny. You

are allowed to do so. It is your version after all. But I might have to try it as well."

"Thanks."

"I'll let you know when I get to Amsterdam."

"Good, I look forward to visiting."

The Warm Springs Roosevelt campus exists mostly as described. A few liberties were taken with details. For example, there is an abandoned camp on site by the lake, but it was not a Boy Scout retreat.

Similarly, the town of Warm Springs is mostly as described. Unfortunately, Mable's Diner does not exist and to my knowledge never has. Other restaurants and stores are there, however.

The Roosevelt campus and Warm Springs are worth a visit, as well as the Little White House. It was an amazing place in its time, and hopefully will be again. The history there is as thick as the scent of magnolias in June.

Kat does exist and will welcome visitors. Kat is not her real name—I've used a pen name for her to protect her true identity. But if you see a fluffy tabico miniature Maine Coon cat eyeing chipmunks in front of the house, you'll know it's her.

Keswick and its surroundings exist mostly as described.

The Lake District is a great place to visit, preferably in the spring or fall to avoid the summer crowds. Whether hiking, biking, or boating, the beautiful countryside invites outdoor activities. Prepare appropriately for the weather.

ABOUT THE AUTHOR

I'm D. Smith, a native Georgian that can't seem to stay in the state for long. Tried a number of states and Europe so far, and lately have settled in Asheville, North Carolina. But I do now have a house on the Warm Springs Roosevelt campus, so soon that will be home.

I've been a lot of things over my work career, but I've put that nonsense behind me. The travel in America, Europe, and Asia was useful as an author. And finally the Ph.D. came in useful—for writing about food.

I now write books and pet cats for fun, since neither pays very well. I'm weaning myself away from social media, but the links below give a little more background and perhaps foreground on the author known as D. Smith.

RECIPE

FLAPJACK, BRITISH

No, not the limp breakfast frisbee. Rather a crispy, tasty oat bar from a few simple ingredients and simple instructions. What could go wrong? Well, a lot can, but don't worry. Substituting ingredients or changing the process won't result in a proper British flapjack. But if you've never had a flapjack in Britain, you won't know it's not a flapjack. What you'll get is still a delicious oat bar, so enjoy and call it a flapjack or whatever you want. The same way we treat scones, croissants, and gelato in the US—maybe they are not what they are in Europe, but they are still good.

The Ingredients
    2 1/3 cups Oats, Quick
    1/4 cup Golden Syrup
    1/2 Brown Sugar
    1/2 cup Butter (1 stick)

The Process

Melt the syrup, brown sugar and butter in a saucepan over low to medium heat. Butter needs to be fully incorporated, but leave some sugar crystals if you want extra crunch.

Remove from heat and add the oats. Stir until fully coated. Dump into an 8x8 greased baking pan. Don't spare the grease or you'll never get them free. Or use baking paper. Bake at 350 F for 20 to 25 minutes. The middle should be soft and the edges firm. Be aware they continue firming while cooling. Cut and enjoy.

Finishing Notes

Flapjacks seem easy, but these bars are so simple they are hard to perfect. Substituting for the golden syrup is a no-brainer, right? Hard to find and expensive, so sorghum, molasses, corn syrup or even honey could work. But change the syrup and change the outcome. Same for the type of oats. Try Quick Oats and stay away from Instant; even steel-cut oats can alter the texture. The brown sugar can also affect the texture. Larger granulated sugar, like turbinado, is preferred to get a little extra crunch if you leave some unmelted.

Whatever happens, the bars should still be good. But don't skimp by using cheap or old butter. That flavor is prominent, so using old butter with a refrigerator smell just won't do.

Add whatever you like. Cinnamon, vanilla, nuts, and chocolate chips are just a few variations found in British bakeries. Think of it as a granola bar and go wild. If you want them crispier, then use a larger pan and spread thinner, or bake longer.

Note: Most of my recipes are loose, as I frequently experiment and encourage others to do so. It can be fun, if sometimes a bit dodgy.

255

BODY IN THE COVE

CHAPTER ONE

Getting shot recently focused me on who pulled the trigger. They would have plenty of additional opportunities, and I'd prefer they did not. After leaving the hospital with my superficial neck wound, Bryan had briefed me on what they had found. It was not much, but was all I had to work with from the shooting itself. My list of known potential suspects was too large to do much with. And as I had told Bryan, the number of potential unknown suspects was even larger. I had made an impression in Warm Springs and Hamilton County, but perhaps not one conducive to my long-term health.

Meanwhile, I had other issues to deal with. Feeding Kat, attending the bookstore, tending the community garden, and buying groceries were just a few of my life's regular requirements. I also had special projects, such as searching for my assassin, finding a way to shut down Benjamin Rawley, and researching the letter found under the cottage that detailed three murders.

It was a nice fall day, so I decided to tackle the easiest

special project. Benjamin Rawley, a long-time flunky working for the state, had decided he did not like me. It was very mutual. But I did not take it personally since he literally disliked everyone in Warm Springs from what I could tell. The feeling was universally mutual. Yet no one had taken a shot at him, so I guess I was less liked than Benjamin. Sobering, but it was an environment I was familiar with due to past actions that usually ended up with me being disliked.

I needed help to get something major on Benjamin that would not allow him to use his powerful friends in Atlanta to continue protecting him. I thought I knew the right person for the job. I drove over to Hamilton, the county seat of Hamilton County. I parked near the courthouse and walked to a small but nice office. There was no longer any sign on the post outside, and a light spot on the building itself showed where another sign had once been.

I was at the office of Lawrence K. Endicott, IV. Formerly called Larry the Lawless because he did not do much obvious lawyering, despite his office's proximity to the courthouse. Instead, his specialty was setting up shell companies and other legal devices for crooks all around the region. Then he was caught with a brick of marijuana and $100,000 in unexplained cash. Knowing he was framed, and likely by one of his clients, he gave away most of his secrets to the authorities. His penance was probation and disbarment; hence, the lack of signs at his office.

I was the one who framed Larry, and I told him afterward. He was not happy about what I had done, but he realized he was leading a brief life, as any day one of his clients, or a competitor of a client, was likely to shoot him. Criminal organizations under investigation for various prior wrongdoings were getting their corporate shells unraveled by the feds. The criminals would not take a chance on Larry flipping on them. Now he had flipped on all of them, en masse, and he was possibly still in danger despite assurances from the state and federal authorities. But altogether he was in a better place with all the stress of his previous life gone. He had inherited the office, money, a house and some land, so did not need to continue earning. But he still felt compelled to visit his office several times a week.

I walked in and sat in a comfortable chair across from his desk. His receptionist had departed immediately after his arrest.

"Hey Larry."

"Hi James. You just happened to be in the neighborhood today?"

"Something like that."

"Did you do the bookstore deal?" Larry asked.

"Yes, and thanks for reviewing the papers. Here is your fee." I opened my wallet and handed Larry a crisp one-dollar bill, his usual fee. It was our joke. He did not need the money, nor could he give legal advice, much less take money for it according to the terms of his case and probation. My giving him a dollar technically broke the rules and stuck a finger under the nose of the broken legal system. The same system that allowed him to work with criminals to set up legal shell corporations, then take the fall once discovered. While the criminals, at least so far, had not been arrested.

"Thank you. I'll put this toward my effort to remain disbarred."

"I thought you would have closed the blinds. Since you don't want anyone to know you are associated with me."

"Just the opposite. I assume anyone following you already knows it. The open blinds give them a clear view of you, so they won't shoot me by mistake. Other than a window repair and a new chair to replace the one you are sitting in, I come out ahead."

"I see your point and can't argue with the logic. But aren't you just as likely to be on a hit list as me?"

"Now it is my turn to see your point. I need to invest in steel blinds to deflect any bullets regardless of who is here with me."

"Would not it be hilarious if we both got shot right now, by different people for different reasons?"

"There is some humor there, but I don't share your enthusiasm for what would be painful for both of us."

"True. But even more painful for your cleaning service."

"I doubt it. They would merely be annoyed, but well paid to clean it up. While we would be dead. Now, to what do I owe the pleasure of your company today?"

"Per our previous conversation, do you have the materials on Benjamin Rawley?"

"I do, but there are complications. You need something to get him fired, so who else do you want to be implicated."

"I would hope no one else. Just Ben."

"That will be tough. All his misdeeds were entwined with others."

"I see. Can you give me a couple of scenarios, names redacted of course, and let me choose one?"

"I can do that. But the fee is double because of the extra work."

"No problem."

"Give me a few days to pry out the good stuff and arrange it."

"I'm not in a great hurry. Thanks."

I drove home and thought about my life lately. Called to Britain to help an ex-wife out with a murder investigation. Only to get involved in a Russian methamphetamine operation. But I got to know her daughter and made a friend. Then I came home to get dumped by my new girlfriend, Donna, and then get shot at by an unknown assailant. And getting partially bought out of my bookstore. My only anchors were my house, a dilapidated cottage, and Kat. But those were all good things. With the bookstore mostly gone, I now had time for those things.

I had already signed the papers, and my bank account had perked up from the partial buyout. The biggest change for me was not working at the bookstore every day. I could take it for two days a week. More if Millard or Lottie were gone, less if I needed time elsewhere. Oh, and Lottie had decided to give it a real name. My meager contribution to the initial documents to open it had listed it as the Warm Springs Bookstore. Lottie felt it needed something more marketable, but she had not decided what it might be yet. I'd leave it to her to come up with something catchy.

www.ingramcontent.com/pod-product-compliance
Lightning Source LLC
Chambersburg PA
CBHW031028310726
48969CB00007B/1904